THE DUKE'S RELUCTANT BRIDE

SWEET REGENCY ROMANCE

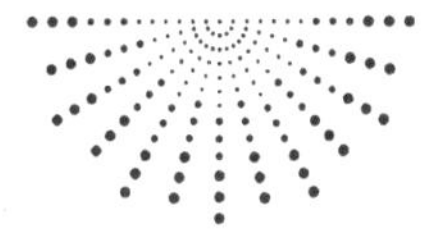

CHARLOTTE DARCY

SWEETBOOKHUB.COM

CHAPTER ONE

Horses were her first love, her second, and her third. In fact, for Charlotte Botley, the company of the equine was preferable to the company of her fellow man and woman. Far preferable. It had been at the tender age of six that her father, Sir Cyril Botley, had placed her tentatively upon the back of a horse called Buttercup and trotted her gentle around the stable yard. Little did he know the fascination he had unleashed and now, at the age of twenty, Charlotte's love of horses had turned almost to the point of obsession.

She lived her life with little thought for anything else. Since reading of Monsieur Claude Bourgelat's school of veterinary medicine in a periodical some years previously she now harbored only one desire. Charlotte would practice veterinary medicine and that was final. She had no other ambition save that one hope for which she had devoted so many years of her life thus far.

Her parents had naturally tried to dissuade her, this was not the occupation for a young lady. Needlepoint would be much more suitable. She was, her father and mother reminded her, a lady of considerable means, possessed of rank and fortune. She lived in a rural idyll, a district of Hampshire noted for its fine society and well to do people. Women such as her did not concern themselves with the more delicate aspects of horsemanship. That was a matter for grooms and stable boys. A horse was for riding, side saddle, and with decorum. Its purpose was to bring a lady to her destination and back again, not to be examined and poked.

Just like she had, her father declared the matter to be settled. Imagining it so, her mother had encouraged her to find a husband and made steps towards such arrangements at an alarming rate. Ever since her eighteenth birthday, Charlotte had been subjected to a string of interminable dinner parties to which the dullest and most vulgar of men were invited. These 'aristocrats' had shown little interest in anything she had to say, preferring instead to see her as a prize to be worn upon their arm. They treated her accordingly.

On her part, Charlotte had done her best to dissuade them and had been largely successful, much to her mother and father's annoyance. They were adamant that she should find a husband and she was adamant that she wished only to practice veterinary crafts while spending her time in the stables or out riding. A stalemate was established, one where neither side was willing to back down. Charlotte ordered books on the anatomy of horses and the treatment of colic and other disease whilst her mother wrote out endless invitations to would-be suitors, assuring them that her daughter was the most suitable proposition.

It seemed that nothing could be done to break the stalemate which rested over Goodnell Manor, the home in which Charlotte's love for horses had first been kindled in the impressive stables which her grandfather built in the grounds many years before. She was, her father said, an unfortunate product of his influence from beyond the grave, the house being filled with all manner of art and sculpture related to equine pursuits. It was from him that Charlotte had inherited her love for horses and how sorry she was that she had never met the man who would surely have understood her the best.

～

Charlotte had forgotten entirely about the luncheon, so engrossed had she been in the latest volume to arrive from London. Mr. Hatchard, of Piccadilly, knew well of her love for all things equestrian and he had made a point of sending down a list of his newest acquisitions each month, a list which Charlotte was all too pleased to receive.

Currently, she was reading a book of anatomy, with a most marvelous set of pictures. Bent over her desk she had made several copies in the course of the afternoon, eager to memorize precisely the intricate details. She wanted to know everything she could and was busy writing out a list of the Latin names given to the anatomical parts when the door to the library opened and her mother, Lady Louisa Botley, appeared with a letter in her hand.

"You missed your luncheon, Charlotte. The bell was sounded three times. I did suggest that we send the maid to call you, but your father was insistent that we begin. There is a little soup still in the tureen if you are hungry?" Lady Louisa said, in her sing-song like voice.

Charlotte's mother was the epitome of kindness, some ten years younger than her father, she had always been more of a friend than a mother to Charlotte. However, she simply could not understand her daughter's obsession with animals. Charlotte had tried her best to explain but her mother's interest lay purely in the social and she could not for the life of her understand why any young woman would not delight in an eternal round of balls and soirees, theatre trips, and picnics.

"I am not hungry, thank you, ma'ma," Charlotte said, looking up briefly at her mother, as she tried to remember the term for the Gaskin and where the Coronet began.

"But you cannot pour over these books all day, Charlotte, you must get ready for this evening," Louisa replied.

Charlotte looked up with a curious expression. "This evening?"

Her mother sighed. "The dinner party, Charlotte. I have just received the final acceptance from Lord Palmer. Do you not remember?"

Charlotte gave her a look to suggest that she most certainly did not.

But the announcement of a dinner party was hardly unexpected. Her mother held one almost every week and the procedure was always the same. At six o'clock the guests would arrive, sherry would be served, and introductions made. Sometimes the guests would be familiar, for a district like that around Goodnell Manor could only be expected to produce new fruit occasionally. But often, an outsider would be found, a guest of some notable person or an acquaintance all as interminably dull as the last.

Charlotte would be forced to sit through the soup course at the right hand of some boorish rake before spending the fish course at the hands of the gentleman to her left. When the sorbet was served her cue would come to change to another seat at the table where the same procedure would be enacted again. She would feign an interest in social matters, poetry, the local ladies and for the gentlemen the pursuits of hunting – which she was entirely against. Then they would talk of the latest scandal and gossip to come from town and endure the main course in the knowledge that more was to come.

By the time that the pudding was served and her mother made the announcement that the ladies could retire to the drawing room, Charlotte could have endured the attentions of four or five different men, all of whom believed she had an interest in them. The fact that she did not hardly seemed to matter. At the end of it all, her mother would pronounce the evening a complete success. Informing Charlotte that she looked forward to hearing which of the men she might choose to meet again. Thus far, her mother had been disappointed. Charlotte would return to her books, making a comment as to the unsuitability of each of the men in turn and would consider the matter to be settled. It was a perpetual ritual and one which would be repeated that very night.

"Ah, a dinner party, how delightful," Charlotte said.

This time her mother sighed. "One day, Charlotte, you are going to have to take things seriously. You cannot live your life surrounded by piles of books and without any consideration for your future. Surely you must see that, dear?" Louisa said.

"But they are always such awful men, ma'ma." Charlotte still had her head buried in her book.

"To whom you never even give a chance. What about Harry Williams? He was a delightful boy, was he not?" Louisa asked.

Charlotte groaned. "He was a complete bore. All he spoke of were his connections at court," she replied.

"Or Vaughan Clark, Sir Harry's son," Louisa continued, clearly choosing not to dwell upon the negatives.

"A man already possessed of a gambling addiction at the tender age of twenty-three and in serious need of both a tailor and a valet," Charlotte said.

"Well, I have invited several gentlemen to join us this evening. Lord Palmer, from whom I have just received word, James Corbett, a most successful businessman rumored at eight thousand a year and a young man by the name of Percival Wentridge, an up and coming gentleman in civil law. You are bound to like one of them." Louisa didn't look entirely firm in her conviction.

"I doubt it," Charlotte replied.

"Oh, Charlotte. Why will you not be like other girls of your age? I have invited Honoria too so that you may have some company once the gentleman retire."

At this. Charlotte looked up with a smile. Honoria Fitz was Charlotte's closest friend, though she was in just as much cahoots with her mother over Charlotte's matrimonial arrangements. Still, it would be fun to have her there and Charlotte was grateful for this one thing which might make the evening a little more bearable.

"And for that, I thank you, ma'ma," Charlotte said.

Louisa's face softened into a smile. "I only have your best interest at heart, Charlotte. I long for you to find a man to love you, just as I found your dear father."

"But I do not crave such a match. I am content to live as I live and to hold my ambitions in my heart as you do your love for my father," Charlotte replied, wishing that her mother could only see that her ambitions lay elsewhere.

"But you are such a pretty young lady, Charlotte, your blonde hair, your blue eyes, your slim figure. Why waste all of that on a horse?" Louisa's voice now bore a note of exasperation.

"It is not merely one horse, ma'ma. There is so much that I love about the equestrian arts and I want to know everything I possibly can about them. I am determined to realize my ambitions and to enter the veterinary school in London. I am certain that I am nearly ready to take the examination," Charlotte replied.

"But a young lady should not concern herself with such things. Those examinations are for men. For those who would work in the stables of great houses or of the Regent himself. There is no place for a woman there." Louisa's face displayed her usual horror at the thought of her daughter participating in such an astonishing occupation.

"And why should I not be the first?" Charlotte asked.

It was her only dream, the dream she had possessed since childhood. An ambition that had only grown since its first flourishing, despite her mother and father's best attempts to stop it.

"Oh, well, I do not know, Charlotte. You seem entirely determined but you know your father will never allow it. He tolerates your activities here, but to think of your going off to London in pursuit of such a thing is beyond our imagining. No, you must stay here and find a husband. Now, do not spend too long in the library, you have a dinner to prepare for." Louisa smiled at Charlotte, before closing the door behind her.

Charlotte rolled her eyes. It was no use arguing with her mother, her mind was entirely made up. Charlotte would marry and that would be an end to the matter. But Charlotte had other ideas and no desire to find a husband. It was not that she was averse to such a thing, the thought of marriage often crossed her mind. But it was not her preoccupation, as it was for many of the young ladies in the district.

She knew there was jealousy on the part of other women who lived nearby. Jealousy that Charlotte should be possessed of such good looks but fail to take advantage of them. They simply could not understand why a woman with so many suitors could find so many reasons to avoid them, nor could they understand why such a woman should prefer the conditions of the stable to that of the salon. That was why Charlotte kept herself to herself, preferring only the company of Honoria who, though of little understanding as to Charlotte's love for the equestrian, at least did not display her animosity to it openly.

Charlotte smiled to herself at the thought of her mother now seeking out her father and engaging in their usual conversation of lament over her waywardness. Her father would denounce her as a fool, shaking his head in despair and telling her mother that they should have crushed her foolish obsession with horses at its earliest signs. Her mother would wring her hands and blame herself, whilst her father would reassure her that this phase would eventually pass if only she could find the right man, one with a firm hand and one who would not tolerate or indulge their daughter's equine habits.

Charlotte was not about to find such a man, nor had she any intention of allowing herself to be the subject of her mother and father's designs. She returned to her books, flatly refusing to make herself presentable as the afternoon drew on. It was almost five o'clock by the time she laid aside her papers and closed the volume of anatomy. She was a quick learner and had memorized almost half of the terms she had found in the latest diagrams.

"I shall go and see if I can remember them in the stables," she said, rising from the desk and making her way out of the library.

It was a beautiful evening, the sun casting its warm glow over the Manor House grounds, for it was late summer and the days were still long. The stables were her favorite place. She had looked forward to seeing the horses all day, having already visited them earlier that morning at feeding time She could hear the neighing and whinnying from across the courtyard at the back of the house and hurried eagerly into the stable yard where she found her father's groom, Michael Tibley mucking out one of the horses who stood patiently to one side.

"Michael, how is Jet this evening, is his leg any better?" Charlotte asked, as the groom removed his hat and nodded to her.

He was a young boy of nineteen, possessed of a shy disposition and, like Charlotte, happiest around horses rather than in the company of others.

"He is doing well, ma'am, yes. I have rebandaged the

leg as you suggested. He seems to be tolerating it well," he said.

Charlotte smiled. "Good, I read about it in one of my books. The way the bandage is tied means that the animal can still move the muscle and so is in far less discomfort than those rigid bandages we used to use," she said, patting the horse at Michael's side, a chestnut mare named Chaser.

"There is not a thing you do not know about the horses, ma'am," Michael said, smiling shyly at her.

"Oh, but I have so much still to learn, Michael. I have been sat in the library all afternoon trying my best to learn all the names I must remember for these examinations," Charlotte said, mentally recounting the names she had learned as she stroked Chaser's mane.

"It is on instinct by which I tend to them, ma'am. I could never learn such things," he said, shaking his head and smiling.

"Ah, but you know the horses far better than I do, Michael. It is almost as though you can speak to them and they understand you," Charlotte said, for she had always been astonished at how Michael could understand the needs of the horses and the way they responded to him.

"I have always had that gift, ma'am, just as my father had it before me, and my grandfather before him," Michael said.

"Your grandfather and my grandfather were great friends. It was their love of horses which brought them together," Charlotte said, and the groom nodded.

"That and a drop of brandy I think," he said, and Charlotte laughed.

"A pleasure which it would not be fitting for me to indulge in. However, I suppose I must now go and get ready for this evening. My mother has arranged another interminable dinner party, though I would far prefer to remain here," she said, shaking her head.

"The horses will still be here tomorrow, ma'am," Michael said.

Charlotte nodded. "And how fortunate that is, for I would surely go quite mad if they were not," she said, causing the groom to laugh.

"Good evening to you, ma'am," he said, and

reluctantly, Charlotte made her way back towards the house.

"It is just too awful," she said out loud, as she came into the hallway, where the servants were busy carrying glasses and crockery back and forth.

"Are you not ready yet, Charlotte?" Lady Louisa asked, emerging from the drawing room with a look of horror on her face.

"I am about to ready myself, ma'ma," she replied and hurried up the stairs.

The next few hours would be an endurance, one which Charlotte could only have a reprieve from at the thought of the horses. Animals who sought nothing from her but oats and affection, rather than marriage and flattery.

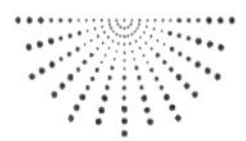

CHAPTER TWO

Charlotte was bored. She was sat between Lord Palmer and James Corbett, both of whom were attempting to outdo the other in their flattery and conversation. Charlotte had little desire to listen to either of them and had almost fallen asleep during the soup course, much to her mother's consternation.

"We are pursuing an interest in the colonies currently, there is great expectation in sugar cane and I hope to be at the forefront of its exploitation," James Corbett was saying, as the fish course was placed in front of them.

"And I too have considerable interests in the

colonies, my brother is there now," Lord Palmer interjected.

Charlotte felt herself as though torn between the two.

The evening had progressed in precisely the manner she had predicted. Her mother had introduced the guests one at a time over sherry and there had been the usual circling and social niceties. Honoria had arrived last, accompanied by her father Mr. Fitz, the rector of Saint Matthew's, the ancient village church. He and her father had talked at length about the changes to the diocesan boundaries and the petty squabbling of the Archdeacon with Lord Ackroyd over the payment of glebe money and they had then made their way to the dining room where the excitement of the conversation had barely improved.

"An excellent fish course, Miss Botley," James said, lying down his knife and fork.

"Yes, the trout has been prepared with interest," she replied, wishing that the same could be said for the company.

"Shall we move around," her mother asked.

Charlotte breathed a sigh of relief, for there seemed little more to be said about sugar cane and the colonies, little more she wished to hear at least.

On the other side of the table, sat Honoria and Percival Wentridge, a young man with a keen face who looked entirely terrified as Charlotte came to sit next to him.

"Good evening again," he said, as the sorbet was placed in front of them.

"Good evening," Charlotte said, turning at once to Honoria who made a face at her.

"Well, you have already dismissed two of the three, what now for the poor gentleman at your side," Honoria hissed, and Charlotte smiled.

"I am always polite, Honoria, you know that," she said, and her friend began to giggle.

"I hear you are a keen reader, Miss Botley," Percival Wentridge said, and Charlotte nodded.

"Books of a certain type," she replied.

"Ah, well, you will certainly be interested to know that I have just finished writing a most interesting monograph on the legal peculiarities of the window tax. Did you know that certain unscrupulous businesses in the city of London have taken to distorting the glass in their windows to avoid the tax?" he said, sounding as outraged as if a member of the party had uttered a blasphemy.

"I did not know that, sir," Charlotte said, realizing that she was to be subjected to an even more interminable ordeal on that side of the table.

As the main course was served she tried her best to feign interest in what the gentleman was saying but his conversation became gradually even duller and it was only when Mr. Fitz raised the topic of a newcomer to the district that her ears finally pricked up.

"A returner really, rather than a newcomer, for he was sent away to school for many years. However, I doubt he is remembered. I know little about him, but he is the nephew of the Duke, may God rest his soul," Mr. Fitz said, wiping his mouth with his napkin.

"Do you know how rich he is," Honoria said with a wink to Charlotte her father blushed.

"Sebastian Clarence is rumored to be possessed of fifteen thousand a year and has properties in London, Derbyshire, and Kent. But it is Glebe Abbey which is the ancestral home. His uncle had no children, no heir, and so it is Sebastian who has inherited the title and the estate. A fortunate man indeed," Mr. Fitz said.

"And he is here in the district already?" Louisa asked, casting Charlotte a look.

Charlotte rolled her eyes, knowing that her mother's mind was now employed in the scheme of how best to extend an invitation to the newly arrived aristocrat.

"I believe so, though I am yet to call at the Abbey. The Duke possessed several unusual ideas regarding the Christian faith." Mr. Fitz grimaced just a little too obviously.

"He was a Catholic, father," Honoria said, smiling.

"As I say, unusual ideas, but I am not sure if his nephew is so afflicted. One should always cultivate such gentlemen," Mr. Fitz said.

Honoria nudged Charlotte in the ribs, as the

conversation now turned to the state of the church roof and the need for repairs, as the possibility of the new Duke was considered in terms of exploitation. Charlotte turned to her and shook her head.

"Do not even say it, Honoria," she hissed, but Honoria could hardly contain her excitement.

"Fifteen thousand a year, Charlotte. I wanted to tell you earlier, but I did not wish to dispel these other gentleman's hopes. But imagine it, you a Duchess." Honoria's eyes growing almost misty at the thought.

"Honoria, I have not even met the gentleman in question, though I have no doubt that I soon will if my mother is to have anything to do with it." Charlotte was shaking her head.

"Oh, but you must, he will be the perfect match for you," Honoria said, to which Charlotte shook her head and stifled a laugh behind her hand. She knew her friend was teasing her, her mother, and the gentlemen at the table.

"I have no interest, Honoria. I am tired of hearing about suitable men. You know my ambitions." Charlotte shook her head as a large slice of peach delice was placed in front of her.

"Horses, only horses," Honoria said, as Percival Wentridge turned to Charlotte and spoke to her.

"I must tell you a little more about my monograph," he said.

Charlotte sighed. Must he really!

By the time that coffee was served, Charlotte's patience had worn thin. She had heard all she wished to about sugar plantations, window tax, and the fortunes of the new Duke of Fitzroy. She had even grown tired of Honoria's company, for her friend seemed entirely obsessed with the thought of Charlotte's marriage and the hope that she might become a Duchess on the simple basis that an eligible Duke was in close proximity.

"I must go and powder myself a little, the evening is still warm." Charlotte rose from the table, just as Percival Wentridge was explaining a further detail on recent window legislation.

The gentlemen rose and Charlotte curtsied, before

making her way quickly towards the door. Once out in the peace of the hallway, she breathed a sigh of relief for she had no intention of returning. She would suffer her mother's wrath the next morning but for now, she was content to have escaped the company. Feeling a weight lifted from her shoulders, she made her way outside, circuiting the house until she came to the stables.

Michael gave her a wry smile as she approached, shaking his head and beginning to laugh. It was a scene played out a dozen times before, for Charlotte often made a habit of excusing herself from her mother's dinner parties and not returning. Now, she had every intention of riding out and feeling the freedom which was stifled in the company of such dull and boring men. Ones whose only thoughts were of business and marriage.

"Did you make it to the pudding, ma'am?" Michael asked.

Charlotte laughed. "I made it all the way to the coffee, but the company was so awful that I could not bear it any longer. Is Chaser ready for a ride out?" she asked.

The groom nodded. "She is, I kept the saddle handy just in case," he said, and Charlotte smiled.

"You know me too well, Michael," she said, as the groom trotted the horse out from its stable box.

Chaser was Charlotte's favorite horse, a delight to ride and as speedy as the wind. Charlotte had helped to birth her as a foal and had watched her grow into the fine young mare she now was. With her sleek chestnut coat and white patched nose, she was one of the most beautiful horses in the stables and Charlotte always found it a pleasure to ride her.

"I think you shall find it a pleasant ride up onto the ridge tonight, ma'am. The sunlight is particularly beautiful," Michael said, as he helped Charlotte up into the side saddle.

"And if my mother comes looking for me you know what to say," Charlotte said.

Michael nodded. "I am to say that you took the horse when my back was turned and I had no chance to stop you," he replied, laughing, as she trotted off across the stable yard.

"And that way it will only be I that gets into trouble," Charlotte replied.

She waved at Michael and urged Chaser on across the paddock and up towards the ridge. Goodnell Manor lay below rolling hills with woods stretching up onto the ridge above. The village of Goodnell was built along the banks of the river which snaked its way through the valley and several large houses lay along its opposite bank. At this time of year, the hedgerows were in full bloom and the wildflowers blossomed in the meadows. It was the perfect evening which to ride out and Charlotte delighted in her freedom as she urged Chaser along at a canter.

She took the lane which led to the village, but instead of riding through she took a side turn leading towards the ridge which would bring her insight of Glebe Abbey. Despite her earlier dismissal of their new neighbor she still felt something of an interest in the subject of a new arrival in the district. The Duke of Fitzroy had always been something of an interesting figure in local discussion and not just for his unusual religion, as Mr. Fitz put it.

He was something of a recluse and Glebe Abbey was surrounded by high walls and lush, sprawling gardens. It was not known what sort of household the Duke kept, and he was rarely seen in the village so that when news of his death was announced few offered their condolences or mourning on his behalf. Charlotte herself had only seen him on several occasions and he had never attended any social gathering to which she had been privy.

As she rode along the lane towards Glebe Abbey she thought back to her afternoon in the library, trying to recall the names of the anatomical parts she had memorized. She could remember the Pastern, the Stifle, the Coronet, and a whole litany of other names to her satisfaction, though there were still several which alluded her. She was entirely lost in thought before she realized that she had come right to the gates of Glebe Abbey itself.

The wall there had fallen into disrepair and to her surprise the gates were open. She had ridden past there many times and always found them to be firmly shut. From the vantage point of Chaser's saddle, she could see the house itself, a fine old building once the home to Augustinian monks. It had a central tower from which three wings protruded, the walls were covered in ivy and wisteria, the windows blank like dark eyes looking out. It seemed a mysterious place, though not without its charms.

It intrigued her to know what the Duke was like. Would he be a recluse like his uncle or a man who would willingly accept her mother's invitation to dine? Her mother was persistent and Charlotte was certain that she would make it her business to receive the Duke, however hard she had to try.

The sun was beginning to set now, the sky turning red and hazy above. Charlotte was about to turn Chaser around and ride back to Goodnell Manor. She had had her fun and no doubt embarrassed her parents terribly. It would be time to put the horses to bed for another night and return to her own. But, at that moment, she saw two figures walking along the driveway from the Abbey.

It was a man and a woman, walking arm in arm. He was young, handsome, with dark hair and fine features and the woman was equally attractive. Charlotte could only presume that it was the Duke and his wife, though Mr. Fitz had mentioned no such companion. They had seen Charlotte too and she felt suddenly embarrassed at having been seen observing them from a distance.

She wondered if she should speak with them, but what would she say? She felt foolish sat there upon Chaser at the gates of Glebe Abbey. Her eye caught that of the Duke, and he nodded to her, raising his hand to the brim of his top hat, as the woman looked on disdainfully. Charlotte replied with a curt nod of her head and turned Chaser on her tail and rode off down the lane from the Abbey and back towards Goodnell Manor.

It had been a most interesting evening and she looked forward to telling Honoria that she had seen the mysterious Duke, accompanied by his wife. That would soon put pay to any suggestions of invitations on her mother's part and intimations of matrimony on that of Honoria. Charlotte patted Chaser's mane and smiled.

"No, Chaser, I think I shall be quite content with you and your friends as my companions. I need no man to make me happy," she said, as the stables of the Manor came in sight and the evening turned to dusk.

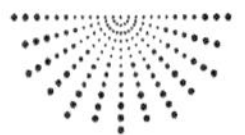

It amused Charlotte to be the subject of her mother's displeasure at breakfast the next morning. Lady Louisa was the kindest and gentlest of creatures and, though she did her best to be cross with Charlotte, it was a charade that she could not long bear to hold. They had sat in silence at first, each knowing the other's thoughts, before the arrival of Sir Cyril who helped himself to eggs from the tureen before making his own thoughts upon the matter more than clear.

"You embarrassed your mother last night, Charlotte. Why must you insist upon running off like that at the end of dinner? It is always the same, you show yourself utterly bored by the proceedings and then disappear. Your mother's guests were most perturbed," Cyril said, vigorously buttering a slice of toast.

"It's because I was utterly bored by the proceedings, father. I heard about nothing except sugar plantations and window tax," Charlotte replied, rolling her eyes.

"Things which will make this country great," he retorted.

"And bore me into an early grave. Percival Wentridge had nothing to speak of but himself. If he were a great adventurer or a soldier or a lion tamer then I should have enjoyed listening, but a lawyer who takes excitement over the particulars of bricked-up windows... that is not someone whom I would wish to spend any longer than I was forced to," she replied.

"But surely one of them was suitable," Louisa asked, an imploring note entering her voice.

"I do not need any of them to be suitable, ma'ma. I need only to be allowed to make my own choices and save you the outpouring of so much distress," Charlotte replied, as her mother sighed.

"We have tried our best, Charlotte and you have thwarted us at every turn," she said, trying her best to look cross.

But her mother could not look cross, even with her best effort and instead, she let out another sigh, just as the maid entered the room and announced that Honoria Fitz had come to pay Charlotte a visit.

"An early call," Sir Cyril said, but Charlotte was pleased to be given an excuse to leave the company of her mother and father and so, rising from her place, she hurried out into the hallway.

There she found Honoria with a stern expression on her face and ushered her into the morning room before she could speak.

"I suppose you have come to tell me that I am a rude and wicked person with no regard for the feelings of men?" Charlotte said.

Honoria's stern face broke into a smile. "Oh, Charlotte, you are such a fool and in fact, I came to chastise you for leaving me alone in their company. I am now an expert on sugar plantations and could write my own monograph upon window taxation — if I should so choose," Honoria said, tutting, as she settled herself down in a chair by the window.

Charlotte sat at the pianoforte and played a string of notes, before closing the keys and laughing.

"But you must admit that I had clearly had enough of the company. It was awful, Honoria and you know it," Charlotte said.

"Well, they will not be returning. Percival Wentridge's face was a picture when he left and Lord Palmer was furious," Honoria said.

"Then I have successfully evaded the attentions of three more gentlemen of this district. Surely, we shall run out of them soon. No one will want to marry me," Charlotte replied, as Honoria shook her head.

"Ah, but there is still one left," Honoria said, looking at Charlotte with a mischievous smile.

"And who do you propose?" Charlotte asked, fearing that she already knew the answer well enough.

"The new Duke of Fitzroy, Sebastian Clarence. The one we spoke of last night at dinner. We must call upon him, that is why I have come so early. We can walk up to Glebe Abbey now and introduce ourselves. You are the daughter of Goodnell's most prominent gentleman, and I am the daughter of the rector, it is our duty to call upon him," Honoria said, folding her arms.

Charlotte smiled, it was hardly their duty to make acquaintances with aristocrats on behalf of their fathers. Besides, she had already seen the Duke, a fact which she would now take some delight in revealing.

"But I have already seen him," Charlotte said.

Honoria looked at her in astonishment. "When?" she asked.

Charlotte smiled a little satisfied smile. At last, she could get her own back. "Last night, as I rode out. I saw him and his wife, they were walking in the gardens and seemed little inclined to be disturbed."

Honoria looked entirely defeated in her plans, but her face suddenly brightened, and she rallied again to her own cause.

"His wife? Well, if he is married then he will surely have a brother, a man like that always has a brother. We must visit and ascertain it. I am sure that the Duchess will be seeking the company of other like-minded women in the district," Honoria said, causing Charlotte to laugh again.

"And what makes you think that we are 'like-minded women' to her," she asked.

"Of course we are, how could we not be? Goodnell is not London, she will be used to high society, to salons and soirees, to fine conversation and sophistication. Now that she is stuck here at Glebe Abbey, she will surely be desperate for company. That is where we shall step in and provide it. Then we shall meet the brother or perhaps both brothers and all shall be well for us. I have always imagined myself with a title," Honoria said, examining herself in the mirror which hung over the mantelpiece and causing Charlotte to laugh.

"You certainly enjoy a flight of fancy, Honoria. We have no notion of these brothers nor that our company will be welcomed. The Duke will be just like his uncle, a recluse, and a man who wishes only for seclusion. The two of them made no attempt to greet me last evening as I rode past," Charlotte said, thinking back to the two figures watching her from along the Abbey drive.

"And given your earlier display, I doubt you made any effort to greet them either, Charlotte. But do come along, it will be fun, great fun, and a perfect excuse to see the Abbey, even if our reception is less than warm," Honoria said, and she danced over to where Charlotte was sat at the pianoforte and took her by the hands.

"Very well, I shall have no peace until I do, that much is certain," Charlotte said, smiling at Honoria, who led her out into the hallways.

"Ah, Honoria, dear," Charlotte's mother said, as they met her in the hall emerging from the dining room, "I see you have managed to drag Charlotte away from her books."

"Do not worry, Lady Botley, she remains in disgrace for her appalling behavior last night," Honoria said, winking at Charlotte.

"And so she should," Sir Cyril said, emerging behind his wife with raised eyebrows, "it was a disgraceful manner in which to behave."

"I am taking her to call upon the Duke of Fitzroy, I am certain there will be an eligible brother or two about the place. She might yet find the love we have been seeking for her," Honoria said, for it seemed that her romantic visions knew no bounds that morning.

"Ah, splendid, I have written to the Duke and made my introductions. I told him that I hoped he would be a more present member of the local society than his uncle and that he is always welcome here at Goodnell Manor. Make your introductions, I have no doubt he will be amenable," Charlotte's father replied.

"You see, Charlotte? We all agree. Now, put on your best bonnet and follow me. We will walk, you will not catch me anywhere near any of your horses," Honoria said, and with that, she led the still reluctant Charlotte out of the house.

The morning was bright and breezy, clouds skidding across the skies above, and the leaves were blowing in the breeze. The two women made their way towards the village, turning at the lane which led to Glebe Abbey and chattering happily together as only the best of friends can do.

"He seemed an unfriendly sort," Charlotte said, as the top of the house came into view over the wall which ran around the Abbey gardens.

"But you said yourself that you did not even speak with him. He was no doubt surprised to see you as was his wife. It was late in the evening and one hardly expects to see a woman riding side-saddle outside one's estate at such an hour," Honoria observed, as they came to the Abbey gates.

They were swung open, the driveway sweeping up towards the house with no sign of anyone save for a gardener cutting topiary in the distance.

"I doubt they will welcome our calling upon them," Charlotte said, thinking that she would far rather be about her studies than paying unwelcome visits to newly-arrived aristocrats.

"Oh, come on, Charlotte. We are here now," Honoria said, taking Charlotte by the hand and leading her up towards the doors of the Abbey.

Charlotte knew there was to be no arguing with her friend and instead she looked up with interest at the imposing building. It was once the home of simple monks and now the home of grand aristocrats and their wives. She wondered what the Duke was really like, for she had been too quick to judge him by a brief encounter and would at least give him the benefit of an introduction if it were the case that they were even admitted.

Honoria was not shy in her approach, she rang the bell, which seemed to echo through the house behind for some time before ceasing. They waited several minutes before footsteps approached and the door was opened by a liveried footman who looked them up and down with a mixture of surprise and disdain.

"We are here to call upon his Grace," Honoria said, presenting her calling card and that of Charlotte.

"Do you have an appointment?" the footman asked.

Honoria shook her head. "One does not need an appointment to make a polite call upon one's new neighbor. I am the daughter of the rector and my friend is the daughter of Sir Cyril Botley," Honoria said.

The footman nodded and ushered them into the entrance hall, which seemed to be a shrine to Glebe

Abbey's previous occupant's love of hunting. Its walls were covered in a large number of exotic heads and skins, a theme continued by the propensity to statuary and icons in keeping with the family's Catholic inclinations.

"Goodness," Charlotte whispered, as the footman went off to ascertain their entry.

"I have always wanted to come here, I had heard about all this, but never dreamed it was true," Honoria said, still gazing around her a little wide-eyed.

"They must be quite eccentric," Charlotte said, just as the sounds of the footman returning echoed into the hallway.

"His Grace and her ladyship will see you now," he said, turning on his heel and marching back along the corridor from which he had just emerged.

"Surely he means the Duchess?" Honoria whispered as they hurried after him.

They were led along a wide corridor, lined with further eccentricities and grand pieces of furniture. There were portraits of the former Dukes alongside exquisite pieces of religious art and tapestries depicting the lives of the saints and martyrs. Alongside these were a considerable number of paintings and drawings depicting horses, there was even a horse's head, preserved in all its glory, almost as real as any in her stables. It was quite astonishing, and Charlotte marveled at it all.

"Is the Duke an admirer of the equine?" she asked, as they arrived outside a large and imposing door, the footman made no answer and simply wrapped three times for entry.

They were ushered into a large and well-furnished room, in which a fire burned merrily in the hearth and a lady and gentleman, the same which Charlotte had observed the evening before, sat waiting. They were well dressed, with the air of aristocracy about them, the woman looking with some curiosity at them, as the gentleman rose.

"Miss Charlotte Botley and Miss Honoria Fitz," the footman announced, and both women curtsied.

"I am pleased to make your acquaintance," the Duke replied, bowing to them, and ushering them to sit.

"The pleasure is ours, Your Grace. We have come to

introduce ourselves and welcome you to Goodnell," Honoria said, pushing Charlotte forward, as both women blushed and curtsied again.

"And this is my sister, Lady Emily Clarence," the Duke said. The woman nodded.

She was pretty, though her face had not yet broken into a smile or any other expression except for slight annoyance at this unexpected interruption.

"Your sister, sir, we thought ..." Honoria began, and the woman huffed.

"You thought we were married, that I was the Duchess and that I would be perpetually bored in this rural backwater without the company of likeminded women," she said, causing Honoria to blush even further.

"Well, we only thought to make ourselves known," she began.

The Duke shook his head. "You will forgive my sister, she means no offense by her words. But we are often mistaken for man and wife and it can become tedious. I am glad you have called upon us," he said, smiling at Charlotte, who nodded.

He really was a most attractive man and the news that he was unmarried was certainly not a disappointment, though Charlotte knew it would now be further fuel for Honoria's ideas. They sat down opposite the Duke and his sister, an awkward silence now descending.

"Do you intend to remain at Glebe Abbey or will you return to London?" Honoria asked, finally breaking the silence.

"Ah, well, Glebe Abbey has its charms, though my sister would be happier in town, would you not, Emily?" the Duke replied.

"I like the countryside perfectly well, thank you," his sister replied.

Charlotte wondered why she seemed so standoffish towards them. She barely spoke a word during the conversation, though the Duke seemed amiable enough, friendly, if somewhat bemused by their presence. Charlotte knew it had been somewhat of an oddity to call upon him in such a way, though she could not possibly have resisted Honoria's insistence that they do so.

"You are engaged to be married?" Honoria asked

after they had discussed the social makeup of the district and she had commented critically upon the furnishings of Glebe Abbey, which, she said, were far from her taste.

"Honoria," Charlotte whispered, blushing at her friend's boldness.

"No, I am neither engaged nor courting," he replied.

Honoria let out a shriek of delight. "How wonderful... I mean, not for you but for... well, it is such a shame," she said.

Charlotte felt entirely embarrassed.

"And now we see the reason for their visit, Sebastian," Lady Clarence said, suddenly rising from her chair. "It is always the question which young ladies ask of you and now that you are titled they will ask it even more."

"Emily, please, let us not discuss this now," the Duke replied, and his sister sat back down and folded her arms.

"Perhaps it is time that we made our departure," Charlotte said, glancing at the Duke, who smiled and laughed.

"Please, do not leave on my account, but then might I ask if either of you are courting presently?"

Honoria let out another involuntary shriek of delight. "No, well, I am not, but then what do I matter? Charlotte is not, not at all, she never has been, she is entirely unattached," Honoria said, as Charlotte took hold of her arm and dragged her towards the door.

"Forgive us we should be leaving. I have no intention of courting, none at all. I have my own plans thank you for your hospitality, Your Grace, Lady Clarence, good day," she said, as both women affected a curtsey at the door.

"Well, good day to you," the Duke said, looking ever so bemused, as Charlotte and Honoria took their leave.

It was only when they had successfully navigated the corridors of the Abbey and emerged from the hallway and onto the forecourt that both women burst out laughing and Charlotte turned to Honoria, shaking her head.

"Really, Honoria, did you have to be so bold? We had barely spoken for half an hour and you have already turned his sister against us and made certain that the Duke shall never wish for our company again," she said.

Honoria only laughed. "He was enchanted by you, did you not see how he looked at you?" she said, and now it was Charlotte's turn to laugh.

"I saw the way he looked at two foolish girls who have entirely embarrassed themselves," she replied.

"But at least we know now that he is a man of freedom, unattached and not taken. He would be the perfect match for you, Charlotte," Honoria said, as they emerged from the gates of the Abbey and made their way back along the lane towards Goodnell.

"And what makes you think that he wishes for a match, Honoria? Or that I am willing for one to occur? He may be precisely as I am and find pleasure and solace in something other than the ways and intrigues of local gossip. Come now, I have had quite enough of all this," Charlotte said, shaking her head.

"Oh, Charlotte, you are no fun," Honoria replied.

But Charlotte had had quite enough fun for one day and was more than content to return home. For a horse cannot embarrass one, nor can it be a foil to one's emotion, and she was more than content with her horses.

But if Charlotte believed the matter with the Duke to be entirely settled, the introductions made and his entry into the district complete, then she was sorely wrong. Upon their arrival at Goodnell Manor, Honoria took it upon herself to inform Sir Cyril and Lady Louisa that they had been entirely mistaken about the Duke and that he was a man without attachments, ready and eager to court.

The fact that the Duke had made no such intimation hardly seemed to matter. Charlotte's mother began to make immediate preparations for a dinner party. One to which the Duke and his sister would be entertained as guests of honor. Not wishing to shirk his own responsibilities, Sir Cyril decided to pay his own visit to Glebe Abbey that afternoon, and thus it seemed that Honoria had unleashed a social whirl, one which Charlotte would find it hard to extract herself from.

"You see what you have done now?" Charlotte whispered to Honoria, who was delighting in having created such an opportunity for her friend, or so she saw it.

"I have merely opened up the possibility," Honoria replied, as she bid Charlotte farewell, informing Lady Louisa that there was every hope that this time things would be ever in Charlotte's favor.

"I feel it too, Honoria, dear," Louisa said, the two women entirely over-excited by the simple news of the Duke's single nature.

Charlotte bid Honoria farewell and excused herself to take refuge in the library, watching from the window as her father made his way down the drive towards Goodnell. It remained to be seen what he might say to the Duke, though she could only imagine the words he might use. No doubt he would tell their new neighbor of his daughter's penchant for the equine and how she would be far better employed in the gentle pursuits of womanhood.

Charlotte sighed, opening her volume of anatomy and beginning to read. It was in this that she found solace, able to escape into a world quite different from that which her parents wished for her. She had no desire for marriage, no desire to court or be courted. All that Charlotte wished for was her dream of attending the veterinary school and putting all she had taught herself into practice.

"I shall do it, and nothing will stand in my way," she said out loud. Though she knew it would be difficult, it was a vow she intended to keep.

It was two days later, and Charlotte had purposely avoided the subject of the Duke in the company of her father and mother. Sir Cyril had paid the gentleman a visit and claimed to have been warmly received, though less so by Lady Clarence who it seemed reserved her steely gaze for any visitor to Glebe Abbey.

"A most charming gentleman," Sir Cyril had said.

"And did you press the matter of Charlotte's necessity," Lady Louisa asked, as the three of them took tea.

"Necessity?" Charlotte shook her head but her father made it clear that the Duke was well aware of Charlotte's 'necessity.'

"I have no necessity, no need of a husband," Charlotte replied, before stalking off to the library.

Since then, she had done her best to avoid both of her parents, knowing that the matter of matrimony would soon arise in almost any conversation. She had found solace in the stables, particularly in the company of Michael, who had been teaching her more about grooming, an art which had so far eluded her, though was no less important in keeping the horse healthy. He explained how it gave him the chance to check over the animal's body. Looking and feeling for changes that might develop and therefore treating anything early.

"You see, Chaser here has such a sleek coat, ma'am, but she needs to be brushed every day, else it shall become matted," Michael said, as he and Charlotte brushed the horse down, her sleek coat looking so attractive in the afternoon sun of the stable yard.

"I have groomed horses since I was a child, but I do not know how you manage to keep her so still. I wish I had your way with the horses. They seem to delight in ignoring me at times," Charlotte said, sighing, as Chaser turned her head away and nuzzled into Michael.

"I spend every moment of the day with them, ma'am. Forgive me for saying it but they know me, that is why. There is no doubt in your sincerity towards them, you love them as much as I, but some people have that gift with the horses, the whispering they call it. Everyone in my family has had it," Michael said.

"My grandfather had it too, just as yours did, but I wonder if I shall ever discover it for myself," she replied, sighing and laying aside her brush.

"Perhaps," he said, patting the horse's mane.

Charlotte went off feeling somewhat dejected. She could learn everything possible about the horse from her books but if she could not have that same affinity with which Michael tended them, she could surely never truly be that which she wished. Still, she had the determination and if she had to spend every waking moment in the stables then she would do so.

It was to her immense surprise that Charlotte returned to the house to find her mother in a state of nervous excitement, pointing towards the library door and clutching her hands together in delight. Charlotte knew at once that something of intrigue had occurred and she was even more surprised to see the calling card of the Duke of Fitzroy lying on the hallway table.

"He has come to see you, Charlotte, be quick now, I was just about to send the maid to find you. Your father is entertaining him, hurry along now," Louisa said, and with no time to protest, Charlotte was thrust into the library.

There, she found her father and the Duke engaged in conversation, the latter rising to greet her as soon as she entered the room.

"Ah, Miss Botley, your father and I were just

discussing you in the most glowing of terms," the Duke said, causing Charlotte to blush.

"I see," she said, as her father, rose and patted her on the arm.

"I shall leave the two of you alone," he said and hurried from the room.

Charlotte was left alone with the Duke, who continued to smile at her, pointing towards the chair opposite him.

"Miss Botley, your father has made a most persuasive case in your favor," he said, and Charlotte looked at him with some confusion.

"I am not sure I follow you, Your Grace," she replied, sitting primly down and neatening her dress. How she hoped it wasn't too grubby from the stables... or maybe she should hope that it was.

"Well, I knew your father's game as soon as he called upon me. He was even less subtle than your dear friend Miss Fitz, whose father I understand gives the most interminable sermons," the Duke said, causing Charlotte to laugh.

"It would not be my place to comment, Your Grace,"

she replied, though it was well known that Mr. Fitz was hardly the world's most captivating orator.

"Your father has offered your hand in marriage, should I wish to accept it. A bold move, but one that I am interested in pursuing," the Duke continued.

Charlotte's mouth fell open, she was somewhat taken aback by his affront.

She had barely met him only once and she had no intention of marrying him, that was for certain.

"But Your Grace..." she began, and he raised his hand and smiled.

"Do not worry, Miss Botley, I mean nothing by it. It was clear that your father was adamant in the matter. He told me that you possess certain flights of fancy concerning horses and the equine and that you have thus far failed to settle down and find anything other to distract you. I too have such pressures placed upon me, for the talk of the family line is never far from our lips at Glebe Abbey... or anywhere else that I go for that matter. How might it be if you and I were to come to some kind of arrangement in the matter? We could be friends and talk of our courtship might be spread, but in truth, we would both know that it was merely a cover so that we might both live a more peaceful life," he said, smiling at her.

Charlotte was entirely taken aback by his words, for they seemed both astonishing and entirely practicable at the same time. It would solve all her troubles and ensure her parents were appeased, at least for long enough so that she might enter the veterinary school. But still, the deception seemed too great, for she did not want to hurt her parents, even though there would surely be some delight in the deception.

"I am not sure, Your Grace. Could we really maintain such a rouse?" she asked.

He laughed. "Why, of course, we could. Think of the sport, you are a lover of the equine, are you not? Think of it in such terms and of the advantages that it would bring to each of us," he said, smiling at her.

"But the horses would remain, my first love, Your grace. I would not seek for anything else. Such an arrangement would be purely in name and I would not seek anything further. Can I rely upon your honor in return?" she asked, still unsure as to the exact nature of his intentions. After all, she knew nothing of him, and it seemed she was placing her trust entirely in his honor.

"Of course you can, the matter is a simple one, so long as we each wish for it to be so," he replied, rising from his chair and bowing to her.

"Well then, the thought is certainly attractive, though not without its dangers...very well, I accept," she said.

"Then the charade shall begin. I think the two of us shall get along well enough and we need only spend that time together which is necessary so as to maintain the appearance of a courting couple.

"And what of your sister?" Charlotte asked for she knew that Lady Clarence may not take kindly to this abrupt revelation.

"I shall see to it that my sister is accepting of the situation, as I am sure your parents shall be too," the Duke replied, and with that, he took his leave.

Charlotte was left alone in the library, mulling over everything which had just been said. She had either discovered the perfect remedy to her father and mother's insistence on her marriage or instead dived headfirst into a sea of dishonesty from which there would be no escape.

"Either way, I shall have my horses," she declared out loud, and with a smile, upon her face, she made her way out to the stables to tell Michael the good news.

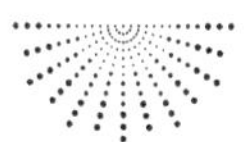

CHAPTER FIVE

In the days which followed, there was great excitement at Goodnell Manor. The news, which came as something of a delightful shock to Charlotte's mother and father, soon found itself disseminated around the district. Charlotte and the Duke were the talk of every drawing room for miles around. There was a sense of collective surprise that the young lady, so resolutely determined never to marry should, in such a short space of time, have found herself matched with perhaps the most eligible man between Goodnell and the capital.

Charlotte played her role with care and consideration, she indulged her mother's constant talk of dresses, carriages, titles, and high society, whilst also keeping her feet firmly upon the ground. Her one ambition was the veterinary school and that had not changed, she had fulfilled the wishes of her mother and father and that was the end of the matter. Honoria too was appeased, though her talk was of little else too, such that Charlotte soon became tired of hearing it and retreated to the library and the stables, the only places where she could find true peace and solace.

"You cannot continue with this foolish idea of the veterinary school, Charlotte," Sir Cyril said, three days after the engagement had been announced.

"And why not? The Duke is perfectly supportive of it, even encouraging. He has done nothing to dispel my enthusiasm." Charlotte was sat at the dining table with a book in hand as she ate.

"But you are to be a Duchess, Charlotte. A Duchess does not spend her time concerning herself with the finer points of equine irritability. She attends balls and parties, hosts luncheons, and undertakes charitable works. She is a model of womanly virtue for her husband's tenants, a good wife, and overseer. It will be your role to manage the affairs at Glebe

Abbey, the servants, and so on. You will have a hundred tasks and all far more pressing than those of the stable," Louisa said.

Charlotte sighed. "Why should I not do both of these things, ma'ma? Why should I be at once one or the other? I am already called upon to see to the needs of the horses in this district, I am known for my skills and I wish only to practice them. Glebe Abbey has run perfectly well all these years without my hand upon its rudder and I am sure it will continue to do so whether I am its dutiful overseer or, as you might put it, neglectful of my duty," Charlotte replied, causing her father to snort.

"Enough of this silliness, Charlotte, enough I tell you," he said, folding his periodical and bringing it down hard upon the table.

Charlotte had no desire to argue with her parents. They would never accept her desire, even, it seemed, now that she had done the one thing they had always longed for. She was engaged to be married, albeit from convenience, and now they still insisted upon controlling the decisions which she made. Well, Charlotte was having none of it and she closed her book, rising from the table and fixing them with a look of annoyance.

"I am going to the stables, it is the only place I can find some peace," she said.

"And what of your husband to be? Should you not pay a call to him at Glebe Abbey? We are yet to even see him here at Goodnell Manor, I have not even had my permission sought for your hand." Sir Cyril shook his head and glowed at her.

Charlotte made no reply, making her way quickly from the dining room with a sigh of relief.

She hurried out to the stables, eager to see Chaser and to hear from Michael on the progress of another horse whose foot had lamed whilst out to ride the day before. There were twenty horses in the stables at Goodnell Manor and Charlotte had made it her business to know each of them as well as she could.

As she came into the stable yard, she could hear Michael whistling to himself whilst mucking out. He had such a natural affinity with the horses, and it was rare to find him ever away from the stables, the horses being his first and his last love. What a simple life it was, one which Charlotte could only long for.

She leaned over the stable door, watching him as he raked out the dirty straw and spread fresh bedding down for the horse, who waited patiently to one side. He did not see her at first, caught up in his work until he turned and looked at her with surprise, as though entirely caught off guard.

"Good morning, ma'am, I did not see you there," he said, his face blushing a little.

"I am sorry, Michael, I stood here and watched you work, I did not mean to startle you. How is the lame horse?" Charlotte asked.

"He is doing well, much improved, and Chaser is eager for a ride. I did not take her out yesterday, but she would enjoy a run, I am sure of it," Michael said.

"Then I shall ride out with her presently. I have just endured another breakfast at which I am told my ambitions are futile and that I should give up any hope of ever attending the veterinary school," Charlotte said, sighing again, as she leaned upon the door.

"Sir Cyril is still not keen upon your taking up your studies in London then?" Michael said as he finished raking out the last of the straw.

"I feel I could do anything but that. I do not know why they are so adamant that I should choose a different path," she replied.

Michael shook his head. "Well, ma'am, you are now engaged to be married, a Duchess no less, perhaps Sir Cyril thinks that such a thing comes with added responsibility," Michael replied.

Charlotte rolled her eyes. "You sound just like my mother, Michael," she said, and he laughed.

"Forgive me, ma'am, I just cannot imagine you married and attached in such a way. You have always been so adamant that you will not marry and that the thought of such a thing is entirely against your ambitions." Michael was looking at her as though he had some suspicion as to her motivations.

"Well, the Duke is... a delightful man, he will make a fine husband," she replied.

Michael smiled. "It was just that he was here this morning, quite early. I was surprised to see him, but he made no mention of you, ma'am," Michael said.

Charlotte looked at him in surprise. "Here? The Duke? In the stables? Whatever for?" she asked.

Michael patted the horse and came to join her in the stable yard.

"He was enquiring after the horses. He wanted to know all about them, I was surprised and quite taken aback. It is not often that we receive such a visitor and entirely unannounced. I asked if he wished to speak to Sir Cyril and he said no, he wanted only to see the horses and that was that. He spoke to me at length and I showed him all over the yard. He was particularly taken by Chaser and said that she was a fine beast and make no mistake," Michael said.

"But he made no mention of me?" Charlotte asked.

The groom shook his head. "And it is not my place to speak of your marriage, ma'am. I am only a groom and I was quite shocked by his appearance. I felt an awful scruffy looking thing, my face was dirty for I had only just risen, but he seemed friendly, charming even, and he assured me he had a great love for the equestrian," Michael said.

Charlotte was entirely confused. It seemed astonishing that the Duke should have come to the stables unannounced and for what reason? He had shown no interest in equestrian pursuits, he had made no attempt to engage her in conversation over her interests or show any delight in a shared love of horses. It was most curious, and she wondered why ever he should have come to Goodnell Manor that morning and not made his presence known.

"Very curious, very curious indeed," Charlotte said.

Michael shrugged his shoulders. "As I say, ma'am, I am merely a groom and it is not my place to make judgments. It did seem odd to me that the Duke did not wish to speak with you though," he said, tilting his head onto one side and looking at Charlotte with a curious expression.

"You are far more than a groom, Michael. You are one of my dearest friends," Charlotte replied, smiling at Michael, who blushed.

"Well, you are kind ma'am, and I hope I have been a friend to you over these years as well. That is why I felt I had to tell you that the Duke paid you a visit. He had asked me not to say anything as to his presence, but I could not withhold such a thing from you," Michael replied, words which Charlotte found even more curious than the simple fact of the Duke's presence.

"But why would he wish to conceal his presence from me? I would gladly have shown him all over the stables and introduced him to the horses myself, it would have been my delight," she said, entirely puzzled as to this odd turn of events.

"I suppose that is a question which only the Duke can answer, ma'am," Michael replied.

"Then it is a question I shall ask him," she replied, determined to discover the mystery of this strange occurrence.

Charlotte spent the rest of the morning assisting Michael around the stables. She groomed Chaser, saw to the bandages on the lame horse's leg, fetched and carried any number of oat pails, and generally found herself in that state of happiness she only derived from such work, a simple life far removed from the worries which lay waiting for her.

But she could not rid herself of the strange thought as to the Duke's visit. Why had he come to Goodnell Manor that day and why did he show such interest in the horses? It seemed remarkable and the more she thought of it, the more she wanted an answer. As the clock over the stable gateway struck eleven, she saddled Chaser and rode side saddle out towards Glebe Abbey.

"I shall give Chaser a good run," she called back to Michael, who waved her off with a cheery grin.

"I shall have some nice oat mash and milk for her when she gets back, her favorite," he called out, and Charlotte smiled.

She purposefully rode in front of the morning room windows, hoping that her mother would spy her from inside. She wondered what her parents would say if they knew that the Duke had been at Goodnell Manor that morning, surprised no doubt to discover his presence and more so to know that he had not made himself know to them.

It seemed pertinent that she and the Duke should ride out together that morning and perhaps she might even discover more of his love for the equine. It had surprised her to know of his interest in such pursuits and she was determined to know more about it. She would ask him to ride out and perhaps then something of this mystery might be solved.

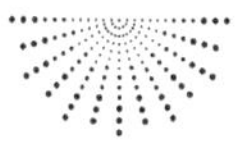

CHAPTER SIX

Charlotte rode slowly towards Glebe Abbey. She paused to admire the view from the lane, the house appearing upon the vista like the rising sun, surrounded by the trees of its parkland. It was a fine house and she wondered what it would be truly like to be its mistress.

She had no desire to be a real Duchess, for she knew that her mother was right. Such a thing came with the burden of responsibility, a responsibility she was unwilling to shoulder. Charlotte knew nothing of such things, despite her mother's best attempts to educate her. She had no interest in such pursuits, nor in learning more of them.

Charlotte was no Duchess in waiting but a woman of

practical considerations. She disliked social gatherings, dinner parties, and balls. Salons and soirees held no interest for her and in conversation, she soon grew bored, unless she were conversing upon a topic she found personally interesting. She would, she declared to herself, make a terrible Duchess, and, as she approached the Abbey it was with such a resolve that she intended to confront the Duke.

She would make it clear to him that their arrangement was precisely that. An arrangement to dispel rumor and gossip. It had thus far been successful in calling a halt to her mother's dinner parties and, she hoped, it had also given the Duke a similar lease of freedom. No longer would they be expected to seek out a suitable match, for there was no doubting that one had already been found. That was the impression she hoped for at least.

But the Duke's arrival in the stables that morning had raised an interesting question. Did they share a common love of the equestrian? And why had he not mentioned it before? Why had he asked Michael to keep his appearance a secret? It seemed a strange thing indeed and, as she climbed down from Chaser's saddle, Charlotte was determined to discover the answer. She tethered up the horse, for there seemed to be no groomsman to hand, and made her way to the door of the Abbey. She was hoping to find the Duke alone, for she had no desire to encounter Lady Clarence. His sister had given only the most cursory response to the news of their engagement and seemed in no way inclined to be civil to her prospective sister in law.

"I am here to see His Grace," she told the footman, who ushered her through the house towards a large sunroom which faced onto the gardens.

It was built of glass and wood, filled with the most exotic looking plants and yet more examples of the late Duke's eccentricities. There, she found the Duke and his sister taking tea. Sebastian rose to greet her, though with something of a stiff formality.

"Miss Botley, you are welcome to take tea with us," he said, indicating to the pot.

Charlotte sat down opposite Lady Clarence, as the other gave her a cursive nod.

"I thought it would be pleasant to call upon you, perhaps we might ride out together," Charlotte said, hoping to elicit a confession of the Duke's presence at the stables that morning from his own lips.

He looked at her with a puzzled expression and clearly had no intention of revealing his earlier excursion. It seemed odd, given his earlier suggestion of friendship and cordiality in their arrangement. If anything, he appeared somewhat uptight and reserved, quite different from his mannerisms when they had been alone.

"My brother does not make a habit of 'riding out,' Miss Botley. We take a walk around the grounds each day and that is quite enough exertion for the day," Lady Clarence said, taking a sip of tea and sitting back in her chair.

The day was already growing warm and, beneath the glass of the sunroom, the temperature was rising. The exotic plants gave off a most unusual aroma, one which perfumed the air and made Charlotte feel almost drowsy. Silence now reigned, broken only by the gentle clink of china, as each of them sipped their tea.

"But it is such a fine day and I thought that Your Grace might enjoy the ride. I have my horse here today, she is a fine beast, Chaser I call her," Charlotte said, attempting to alleviate the mood.

"A pretty name, I am sure," Lady Clarence said.

Charlotte looked at the Duke with a curious expression.

"Perhaps the two of us will take a little walk in the grounds, Miss Botley," Sebastian said.

Charlotte nodded, glad to find an excuse to leave the stifling enclosure of the sunroom.

He led her outside, the two of them walking side by side amidst the rows of lavender plants which grew thereabouts, the sweet scent drifting through the air.

"You do not wish to ride out then? You have no interest, as your sister says, in such a thing?" Charlotte asked, giving the Duke one final chance to reveal his early morning activities.

"I thought that we were to keep our arrangement one of formality," the Duke replied.

"Yes, of course, but on the friendliest of terms," she said.

He turned to look at her with a curious expression.

"This is to be a marriage of convenience, convenience for us both. We should be careful not to blur such distinctions," he said.

"But, sir, my parents already ask why we are not spending more time together. Surely there will be suspicions if it is not assumed that we are as we say we are," Charlotte replied, thinking that at the very least the Duke should make some effort on his part to fulfill his side of their agreement.

"Perhaps, though my sister suspects nothing," he said, glancing back towards the house.

Lady Clarence was watching them from the sunroom, a fact which caused Charlotte to feel somewhat uncomfortable under the gaze unflinching from the window.

"For now, perhaps, but eventually questions will be asked. We must set a date for the marriage, be seen together in public, and at least present as though we were to be married as we claim. Surely a ride out together would allow for such a thing to be noticed," Charlotte said.

The Duke shook his head. "It is of no concern to others how we conduct ourselves. I will not be the subject of idle chatter and gossip as to when and where I am seen and with whom I am seen. That is not a matter to concern anyone but us. No, Miss Botley, the arrangement will stand. You shall have your place at the veterinary school and I shall have the satisfaction of knowing that I am no longer the subject of constant speculation," Sebastian said, glancing back again towards the sunroom where his sister remained watching them.

His words surprised Charlotte, though perhaps they were for the best. She had said herself that she had no desire to be a real Duchess and here the Duke was offering her precisely what she wanted. Still, the matter of his visit to the stables continued to intrigue her and she wondered if she might be bold enough to confront him with the discovery she had made.

"I am content with such an arrangement, though my mother and father still refuse to grant their permission for me to attend the veterinary school or pursue the fancy of doing so," Charlotte replied, as they walked back to the house together.

"But they have no choice in the matter. You are to be married and that makes it your husband's decision. I am quite content for you to pursue your idle fancies if they give you pleasure," he said.

Charlotte furrowed her brow. "Idle fancies? But you share an interest in the equine, do you not? Why else would you have come to the stables at Goodnell Manor this morning and spoken with my father's groom?" Charlotte asked, deciding that boldness was a better hope than caution.

"I swore that boy to secrecy," the Duke muttered under his breath.

"He could not very well keep it a secret. He was curious as to your presence, as was I. That is why I came to speak with you and suggest that we ride out. If we share such an interest then we should do so, if only as friends," Charlotte said, determined to elicit a response.

"My interest was nothing, Miss Botley. I simply wished to be acquainted more readily with my neighbors and, if we are to be married, then it seemed pertinent that I should know more of you. I simply asked the groom for some particulars of the horses and a little knowledge of their stabling, that is all," Sebastian said, evidently annoyed that his early morning excursion had been discovered.

"And I would gladly have furnished you with such information. There is nothing that I do not know about the horses and it would be my pleasure to tell you of them," Charlotte replied.

"I know everything which I need to know now, Miss Botley, thank you," he said, as they came to the door of the sunroom.

It seemed clear that Charlotte was to gain nothing further from the Duke that day. He had made his views clear and he was not about to divulge any further his reasons for visiting the stables that morning. Charlotte would be riding home alone, and she wished the Duke a good day, nodding to Lady Clarence through the window of the sunroom, the woman gave her an icy stare in return.

"Well, Chaser, the mystery deepens," Charlotte said, as she climbed back onto her horse and made her way back down the lane towards Goodnell Manor.

The Duke appeared adamant that there would be no appeasement or let up in his stance. This was purely a business arrangement and one which could still be beneficial to them both. She may yet make it to the veterinary school and the Duke might yet have his peace from chattering society. But there remained in Charlotte something of a question, and she wondered whether or not the Duke really was telling the whole truth about his excursion to the stables and his interest in the horses. It was ever so curious, and she was determined to know the truth.

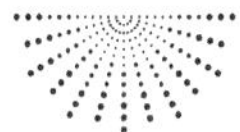

CHAPTER SEVEN

Summer turned to Autumn, the days grew cooler and shorter, a cold eastern wind whipped across the valley and brought with it the first flourishes of snow. It would be a cold winter and there was much talk in the district of them being snowed in for the season.

Such a thing did not worry Charlotte, she had everything she needed, her books and periodicals along with the horses in the stables, her constant companions. She was kept busy seeing to the ailments of many animals in the village, often called upon for her services which were becoming widely known.

Against this backdrop, she and the Duke kept up a pretense of cordiality. She would ride up to Glebe Abbey and receive the now customary reception, cold and distant. Lady Clarence's attitude towards her was growing steelier by the day and the Duke seemed little interested in the pretense of their charade. He was, it seemed, content to be engaged in name only and in little hurry to make such an arrangement official.

But Charlotte's mother had other ideas and whilst subjection to the monotony of her mother's dinner parties was gone it was now replaced by almost constant discussion as to the forthcoming nuptials. When might such a joyous day take place and what arrangements would be made? How many guests, how many carriages, and what kind of dress was she to wear?

It was a conversation that Charlotte had little interest in pursuing. She had no thoughts on such matters and gave little practical input in her mother's questions. She would happily allow her mother to arrange the whole thing and see to it that the wedding passed by as easily as possible. Once she was married, there would be no question of her not attending veterinary school. It would be her husband's choice and that choice had already been made. Charlotte was resigned to follow through with the plan, despite its somewhat unorthodox nature. It excited her to think that soon she would realize her dreams, despite the continuing opposition from her mother and father, who were adamant that the life of a Duchess was a particular one and did not involve work which her father described as being 'for tradespersons.'

"Have you been out again in some dreary stable across the village, Charlotte?" Sir Cyril asked as Charlotte entered the hallway of Goodnell Manor that afternoon.

"It was Mr. Perriwinkles horse, the landlord at The Three Ducks. The poor thing has been lame for two days and he needs to ride out on Saturday to see his sister in the next village. He knew that I could help, and I did," Charlotte said, removing her bonnet.

It was a cold and icy day and her cheeks were rosy and red. She was grateful for the fire in the hearth and made her way over to warm herself, just as her mother emerged from the morning room.

"Charlotte has been out at her... ministerings again," Sir Cyril said, and his wife rolled her eyes.

"Really, Charlotte, you will soon have no time for such things, and then who will the villagers call upon?"

"They will still call upon me, I hope, for I shall make the time," Charlotte replied.

"You should spend your time more wisely, Charlotte. Why not pay the Duke a visit? You have hardly spent any time with him of late. He has dined here only several times and your father and I hardly think we know him. There is still much to arrange and think about before the wedding," Louisa said.

"I see enough of him, ma'ma and, as you often remind me, I am to be a Duchess and I shall spend all my time in his company then. It seems I am to do nothing but the work expected of such a woman, rather than that which I wish to do," Charlotte replied, and without a further word, she made her way out to the stables.

Michael had kindled a fire there to keep warm and he was toasting chestnuts as she approached, looking up at her with a friendly smile.

"How is Mr. Perriwinkle's horse, ma'am?" he asked.

"Oh, quite well now. It was a simple case of laminitis. The horse almost pure thoroughbred and kept on very lush grass and hardly ever ridden. I've explained that he must restrict the grazing and ride the horse more regularly. He will soon be fine, galloping by the weekend, I am sure of it," she said, looking around at her own horses in their stables.

"We are blessed with no injuries or illnesses here, ma'am, and long may it remain. But I heard a strange thing from Dick Pater's boy this morning as I was walking through the village. It seems that His Grace has bought several horses from the farm at Wilkside, they came to the Abbey late last night, a strange thing," Michael replied, shaking his head.

The news was certainly strange, for the Duke had made no mention to Charlotte of his intention to purchase a horse nor of any interest in the equine. But then the Duke had rarely spoken of anything which might suggest mutual or shared interests. He seemed entirely caught up in himself and interested in Charlotte only for her convenience in providing for his own lack of interest in marital affairs.

"It is ever so strange, Michael. Why does he not share his sentiments with me? I am to be his wife and yet he has never spoken of his delight in horsemanship to me, not once. When I try to raise the subject, he is dismissive and I do not dare broach it for fear of angering him," Charlotte said, shaking her head.

"Perhaps he considers it to be a man's place to see to such matters, ma'am... if you will beg my pardon," Michael said, and Charlotte rolled his eyes.

"Then we both know he is mistaken. A woman can understand a horse in precisely the same manner that a man can. It is no different, and he would do well to remember that."

Michael smiled at her, for they both knew that she was right.

"Anyway, I should begin to bring the horses in ma'am. I think we are to have a storm tonight," Michael said, looking up at the sky overhead.

The bright autumnal day was turning breezy now, inky black clouds were gathering upon the horizon and it seemed that Michael was right. There would be rain that night, worse perhaps and Charlotte and the groom began to secure the stables, ensuring that the horses were well bedded in.

"I should stay here myself with them, but my mother and father would only come looking for me," Charlotte said, as they closed in the last of the horses and poured oats into a bucket for it.

"They will be quite all right with me, ma'am. I shall sweep this little fire into a brazier and bring it inside the stable, toast some chestnuts and sit with them," Michael said, as he smiled at Charlotte.

"How I wish my life could be as simple as that," she replied, wishing him a good evening and walking off back towards the house.

She thought again of the Duke, entirely curious as to his actions in buying horses from Wilkside farm. Did he intend to race them? Was it hunting he wished to pursue? Or was he simply a sportsman, interested in the animals purely for themselves? It was a strange thing and one she pondered as she made her way to the dining room for dinner.

The man is so curious, and when will he ever deign to tell me of his life... his interests?

Michael was right about the storm. It struck during dinner, the wind howling around Goodnell Manor, with a squall of rain and sleet battering the windows. The candles on the table guttered in the draught, and Charlotte pulled her shawl tightly around her.

"Goodness me, what a night, and only October," Sir Cyril said, going to the window and looking out over the darkened gardens, just as a flash of lightning lit up the sky.

"It is quite terrible, thank goodness the fire is lit in the drawing room. I shall sit in front of it before bed and keep warm," Louisa declared, rising from her place.

"And I shall go to the library. The fire is still lit there, and I shall finish my book by candlelight," Charlotte said, also rising from her place and making her excuses to leave.

"Then a brandy and smoke are all that will keep me company if the women of the house are to desert me," Sir Cyril said, laughing, as Charlotte's mother took up a candle.

"You know how much I detest these stormy nights. I dread them all summer, knowing that they are to come and not for a moment wishing them to do so," she said, as another draught whipped beneath the dining room door and caused the candle flames to shudder.

Charlotte made another excuse and left the dining room. She made her way to the library, though with no intention of remaining there. Charlotte had other ideas and she slipped on a cloak and stole out of a side door into the storm. She wanted to see the horses and to check that they were well sheltered from the storm. She felt certain that Michael could deal with any problem that might arise, but something now drew her to the stables, a longing to be close to the animals and see them safely through the night.

She had no lamp with her, knowing that it would easily be seen from the drawing room window and arouse the suspicions of her mother. Instead, she made her way across the lawns, seeking out the light from Michael's brazier, which she could see dimly through the stable doors. Another flash of lightning lit up the sky and she could hear the neighing and whinnying of the horses as she drew near to the stables.

"Michael?" she called out, "are you awake? I have come to keep you company during the storm. It is such an awful night."

She had come into the stable yard now, the rain having turned to snow which was blowing in a blizzard all around her and beginning to settle upon the freezing cobblestones. There was no reply from Michael, and she hurried across to the stable door, expecting to find him huddled up asleep beneath a blanket, or lying next to one of the horses for warmth.

But, as she came to the stable entrance, Charlotte was amazed to find the figure of the Duke standing next to the brazier, engaged in urgent conversation with the groom. Both men looked up in surprise as Charlotte appeared at the door, a look of embarrassment now crossing the Duke's face, as Michael stepped forward to usher Charlotte out of the storm.

"Come along inside, ma'am, you shall catch a death of cold out there," Michael said, as Charlotte continued to look with some suspicion at the Duke, who now turned away from her and gazed absentmindedly towards the back of the stables.

She was glad of the warmth from the fire and warmed herself there, pulling off her damp shawl and shaking off the snow.

"We are honored by Your Grace's presence," she said, as the Duke turned to her and nodded.

"I do not have much time, Michael, will you come or not?" he asked, ignoring Charlotte and looking at the groom.

"Well, Your Grace, I am not sure that it is my place to do so. I am Sir Cyril's groom and it is my duty to remain here with the horses at Goodnell Manor," Michael said, causing Charlotte to look at him with even more surprise.

"What is going on here? Why are you here, Sebastian?" Charlotte asked, forgetting all pretense at formality, after all, they were engaged. It was long time that he suggested she use his given name.

"I am here, Miss Botley because one of my horses is dangerously ill. He has cholic and I fear he will not survive the night in such conditions. The stables on my estate are inadequately staffed. I haven't had the chance to find a suitable person and your groomsman here is known for his ways with horses. He has the gift of the whisper, a notable skill," the Duke said.

Charlotte shook her head in disbelief. She could not believe that the Duke was still not willing to admit to her own skills, nor to his own passion for horses. He clearly cared deeply for them, why else would he have come through such a storm as this to bring aid at an hour of need?

"I cannot leave the horses here, Your Grace, my own may become sick with the stress of this storm, and I have a lame horse here to see too," Michael said, glancing at Charlotte who nodded.

"Michael is right, my father would not look kindly on a desertion of duty," she said, eyeing the Duke in the firelight.

"But my poor horse, he will surely die if he is not aided soon enough," the Duke replied.

"And why did you not tell me of your love for horses before now? You knew we shared such a thing in common but instead, you have skulked around and done everything in your power to avoid discussing with me the very matters in which I most delight," Charlotte said.

"This is not the time for this, if you will not come with me groomsman then I must return to Glebe Abbey. May that poor animal's fate rest heavily upon you," the Duke said, striding to the door.

"Begging your pardon, Your Grace, but it is not I who can save the horse, but Miss Botley here. She is the only one who can help you, and she is much more knowledgeable and skilled in the veterinary arts than me," Michael replied.

The Duke's eyes widened and he turned to them with a heavy look upon his face.

"A horse fancier is not what I need," he said.

Charlotte glared at him, hoping her gaze was filled with disdain for the man who behaved like an arrogant fool.

"And that is not what you shall have, Your Grace," she said, pulling on her shawl. "I do not care what you think of me but I will not let a horse die because of your... foolishness." Turning her back she hurrying out into the stormy night.

CHAPTER EIGHT

Together, Charlotte and the Duke made their way towards Glebe Abbey. The storm was drawing in, even more, snow now falling thickly all around and lying in great drifts along the lane. They walked quickly, barely exchanging a word, as Charlotte wondered what she would find in the Duke's stables. He was striding on ahead, as though uncomfortable in her company and she had to almost run to keep up with him.

It annoyed her that he would still not allow her into his confidence nor explain the motivations for his actions. He appeared as a pompous man, who believed that only he could solve his problems and that her presence was neither wished for nor invited.

But Charlotte knew that he needed her and that it would be her and not him who would rid the horse of its fever.

She had gathered several of her instruments from the stables into a bag, prepared for any eventuality which might present itself. Though he hadn't told her what was wrong, from the symptoms she was sure it was colic. A common but sometimes deadly ailment. There had been several cases of it in the village that past year. She knew it was essential to relieve swelling in the stomach, to have the horse walk lest it should roll and twist its gut and to ensure that it took neither food nor drink whilst the affliction was brought under control.

They soon came in sight of the lights of Glebe Abbey, a welcome sight in the snow and Charlotte followed the Duke towards the stables at the back of the house. She had never visited them before, despite her suggestions to the Duke on several occasions and she was astonished by what she found. It was not a simple stable block, but instead, a grand building which must have contained some thirty horses, all stabled for the night. There was no sign of any groomsman and Charlotte looked to the Duke in amazement, as he led her to the far end of the block and pointed through a door, into a stable lit by a brazier and oil lamps hung upon the walls.

"Come now, if you believe your skills can save the horse," he said, ushering her inside.

"Have you no groomsman or stable boys here?" she asked.

The Duke sighed. "I have some help in mucking out during the day, but these are my horses and I would not see them cared for by just anyone. I have not found suitable staff yet and my uncle's stables hands had longs since left. Unless I find the right person, I would rather do it myself. But tonight, I had to admit that my own skills were lacking and that I required further assistance in seeing to this poor beast," the Duke said, pointing to where a bay horse lay breathing heavily on a bed of straw in the corner of the stable.

Charlotte took it all in instantly. Her anger was gone as her training took over. The horse had a distended belly, was sweating and trying to roll. It was colic but they might be too late.

"We have to get him, up," she said as she walked around to the horse's head. Gently she placed her hands on the horse's head, hoping to calm him while feeling for its temperature.

The animal was was damp and clammy, hot, despite the chill of the night and she patted its mane, looking anxiously up at the Duke. As she whispered to the horse it calmed and the Duke came to kneel next to her in the straw. He looked worried, reaching out to place his own hand close to Charlotte's, the horse whinnying as he did so.

"Colic, that much is certain," Charlotte said, reaching into her bag and pulling out her stethoscope. Quickly, she listed to the heart rate, it was elevated but not massively.

The horse groaned and whipped it's head from them as it tried once more to roll. This was dangerous. In this state rolling was a way for the animal to relieve his pain but could result in twisting the gut. If this happened it was fatal.

"What is his name?" she asked as she attached a lead rope to the headcollar.

"Bracken's Chaser, just Brack to me," Sebastian said.

"Okay Brack, she whispered into the horse's ear, we need to get you on your feet."

"What! He is in pain, he needs medicine not to stand."

Charlotte took a breath and stroked the horse, she was amazed at how calm he had become. Colic was a painful and frightening condition, couple that with the storm and she expected that Brack would fight her. Instead, her presence seemed to calm him. Holding his head, she ignored the Duke and looked the horse in the eyes, then she whispered to him that he would feel so much better if he came with her. She knew it wasn't the words she was saying but the gentle and reassuring tone of voice that she had learned from Michael. It seemed that medicine was not just book learning. Gently she pulled on the lead rope and she let go of his head and helped him to his feet.

Brack gave out a groan but he was stoop. For a moment he looked around at his belly and then gave a mournful groan.

"What are you doing?" Sebastian asked.

"As I said this is colic. His belly is distended with

wind. To try and alleviate it he will roll and that is very dangerous. What we must do is walk him gently, keeping him calm. That way the gentle exercise will relieve the swelling and if all goes well he will be fine by morning.

"But what else are we to do about it?" the Duke asked, and Charlotte looked at him determinedly.

"Everything we can. It will be a long night, but I shall not leave this horse's side until he is well," she replied.

The Duke's demeanor seemed to change, his face relaxed into a smile and he nodded his head.

"If you can do anything for him then I would be grateful. This horse is my pride and joy. Brack has been with me for some years ago. It is he who I choose to ride out upon when I wish to escape. He is a faithful friend," he said, patting the animal's neck as they walked.

"Then I shall do all I can to save him."

After they had walked for a while Brack seemed to calm and Charlotte stopped to listen to his side. Loud gurgling was coming from his stomach and he began to paw and stamp upon the ground. The swelling and pain was still there and coaxed him to walk once more. Round and round the stable they went. After about an hour his breathing was a little easier. She stopped walking once more. "We are at a stage where I can release some of the gas," she said and hoped she was right. She had done this only a few times. Colic was usually either fatal or you could walk it off within 30 minutes. They had been walking for longer than that but she knew what she was to try was there best bet. She had done it successfully a few times and only once had she lost a horse. She knew that it was beyond help but that loss still haunted her. "Pass me my bag," she said.

To her surprise, he rushed to fetch it.

"You seem to have a way with horses, Miss Botley," the Duke said, watching with interest, as Charlotte gently inserted a tube up the horse's nostril. It was designed to bring gas from the horse's stomach, expelling it through the nasal passage.

"I have learned as much as I could about every aspect of equine medicine. There is little I do not know about, though I have not had the chance to practice what I have learned as often as I would like," she replied, as Brack stomped his hoof.

"Colic is a dangerous disease. I have lost a horse to it before, several in fact," the Duke replied.

"It is important that the animal does not eat or drink and that the signs are noticed soon, as you have done this night. Sweating, bloating, distress, and uneasiness, these are all signs of the animal's discomfort. But such symptoms can be easily relieved as I am doing now," Charlotte said, grateful that she had had the foresight to bring her medical instruments along with her to the Abbey.

"The horses mean everything to me, Miss Botley. They are like my family," Sebastian said, standing a little closer to her, as Charlotte continued her work.

"And how I wish you had told me of such feelings before," she said, glancing over at him and shaking her head.

It astonished her that he should have kept such a thing a secret, given that it was no secret on her part how much joy she derived from being around the animals and taking care of them.

"There are reasons, Miss Botley. But for now, all that matters is my horse. Do all you can for him and if you can save him then I shall be forever in your debt."

Charlotte nodded. She had every intention of doing so. The horse was already calmer and more relaxed, breathing easily and no longer stomping its feet. She kept her hand upon its neck, gently helping to expel the gas from its stomach, whispering to it all the time.

She had no idea how Michael spoke to the horses, nor whether she was doing so successfully herself. All she knew, was that it seemed to be working. Maybe she had picked up the skill by watching her friend. She would do anything in her power to ensure that the Duke's horse was saved.

The procedure was successful. Now all they could do was wait and hope. Keeping Brack away from any food or water and watching to see if the distention returned. If it did they must walk him immediately, if not then he would make it through the night.

As she stepped away Brack shook his head and walked to the other side of the stable. There he lay down.

"Stop him," Sebastian started.

"It is all right, he is tired but not in distress." She shivered and suddenly realized that she was cold and soaked to the skin.

"You must rush to the house and change and then I will have a carriage take you home," Sebastian said. "I am most grateful."

"Not yet, the immediate danger is gone but it could return, I must stay here until morning."

The Duke stepped out of the stable and came back with a blanket that he draped around her shoulders. The touch of his hand filled her with warmth and as she smiled at him she felt butterflies in her stomach.

"You should go get warm," she said.

"No, but I will send word to your parents and have some hot soup brought to us. There is a brazier just outside, you can warm yourself there and still watch over him."

Charlotte was pleased to do so and she noticed that the Duke's eyes lingered on her a few moments too long before he turned to leave. Once he was gone she felt warmed by that gaze and by the change she hoped these events would bring.

It was the first light of dawn, Charlotte and the Duke had stayed with the horse all night. Brack had soon calmed down and as the hours slipped by his pain eased and eventually, he fell asleep. At that stage, Charlotte had gone to the house where a change of clothes was waiting for her. One of the servants helped her and suggested she stay in the house. Charlotte wouldn't hear of it and when she returned to the stables the Duke ordered them some hot chocolate.

After checking on Brack and finding him still asleep, Charlotte had sat around the fire with the Duke warming her hands on the hot mug. Despite the awful circumstances that had brought them to this moment it was so nice to sit there.

They talked quietly until she heard Brack stir. Rushing to the stable she looked in. The horse was calm and looked entirely normal. Grabbing her stethoscope she listened again to the horse's heart, turning to smile at the Duke, who looked up wearily from his stool.

"I think that he is safe now," Charlotte whispered,

running her hand down the horse's neck and patting him gently on his side.

"And for that, I am eternally grateful. I know so little about health issues, having always relied on others to do that for me. I should learn but one always says that when it is too late," Sebastian said, rising from his place and coming to stand next to the horse, which he patted and fondled.

Brack tossed his head and then rubbed against the Duke's hand obviously enjoying the attention.

"One can always learn, I would be happy to teach you," she said, smiling at him.

He blushed and nodded, his face too breaking into a smile.

"I knew you had a love for horses, Miss Botley, it was clear enough and your groom told me something about it too. He speaks very highly of you, as do others in the district. But I had no real idea of just how knowledgeable you were. You have saved this horse's life, you are a true professional. I have never seen anyone with such skill as you displayed this night," he said, and now it was Charlotte's turn to blush.

"Really, I did nothing, it was a simple case of following what is laid down in my books. Colic can be a nasty thing if left untreated, but there are many steps to be taken so that it might be alleviated," she said, patting the horse's neck once again.

"Then I am in your debt and you have my admiration. I am sorry that I failed to show a proper understanding of your skills. In my foolishness, I had allowed myself to believe your interests were merely aesthetic or fanciful." He shrugged and gave her an apologetic smile.

"My only desire in life has been to enter the veterinary school and my first love will always be the horses," Charlotte said.

"And yet your father still forbids it?"

Charlotte nodded. "He does, though my husband need not," she said, just as footsteps came hurrying through the stable yard.

The first light of greying dawn was breaking over the stables and the snow now lay in drifts all around. A cold wind whipping beneath the stable door and the last glowing coals of the brazier were almost extinguished. Thinking their visitor to be a stable boy, Charlotte turned to issue instructions as to caring for the horse but was surprised to find Lady Clarence now looking with disdain into the stable, as the Duke went over to greet her.

"The horse?" she asked, peering past the Duke towards where Brack stood at Charlotte's side.

"Entirely improved, thanks to Miss Botley," Sebastian said.

"Very well, then we must ensure the animal is well taken care of today. I will have one of the stable boys sit with him. Your work is done here, Miss Botley. You are no doubt eager to return home and warm yourself. You too, Sebastian. I have asked for hot muffins and tea to be laid out in the library for you, a fire is kindled," Lady Clarence said, in a tone which made it obvious that her suggestion was a command rather than an option.

"Ah, well, then you shall see to the horse, Emily?" the Duke said.

One of the footmen is on his way," his sister said. "I am sure that Miss Botley will find her own way home easily enough."

Charlotte nodded, packing up her medical instruments and patting the horse once more.

"Miss Botley, I am in your debt," the Duke said. "I should see that you are taken home."

"There is no need, you must be tired too and the storm has cleared, the walk will be bracing. I will come to visit Brack and you of course," she said, glancing at Lady Clarence.

Lady Clarence's face was set in a scowl. "That will not be necessary," she replied.

Charlotte sighed. "Then I shall take my leave," she said, and with, a final glance back towards the Duke, she made her way across the snowy stable yard and back home towards Goodnell Manor.

"A curious thing," she said out loud, as she paused to gaze back towards the stables. It certainly was strange how the Duke behaved around his sister. As she turned for home once more fresh flakes of snow began to fall.

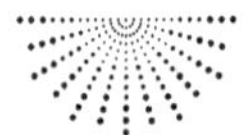

CHAPTER NINE

Charlotte's mother and father were extremely surprised to see her when she arrived covered in snow and shivering for breakfast. They were horrified when they discovered the events of the night before, assuming her to have been safely tucked into her bed as the storm had raged.

"And you went off to Glebe Abbey without anyone knowing it?" her father said, shaking his head and rolling his eyes.

So it seemed that Lady Clarence had not sent word to her home! "If I had not done so then the horse would have died, father," she replied.

Sir Cyril scowled. "Meanwhile, you are willing to risk a fever to save an animal," he said.

"Not just an animal but a living, caring being and the Duke's favorite horse. If we are to be married, then it seemed the least I could do to help him," Charlotte said, helping herself to porridge from a tureen on the sideboard.

"If you are to be married," Louisa said, raising her eyebrows, "there seems to have been little done in preparation for such a happy day."

Charlotte remained silent. She felt confused by the events of the night before, The Duke had been the most delightful company and it seemed his attitude towards Charlotte had entirely softened. No longer had his manner been brash and dismissive, but he had displayed tenderness and affection, that had softened her own feelings towards him as well. But the strange behavior of Lady Clarence still confused her and she wondered why the Duke's sister should behave in such a way, for surely she understood that they were to be married, even if that marriage were not as she might herself be led to think.

"I am going to see Honoria," Charlotte said, having

finished her bowl of porridge and feeling much the better for it.

"But surely you need to sleep, you must be exhausted," Louisa said.

Charlotte shook her head. "No, ma'ma, I am quite all right," she said, and without further explanation, she rose and hurried off to get ready.

She wanted to consult Honoria about the events at Glebe Abbey the night before, to see what her friend might think of her having to endure the steely glances of Lady Clarence. Honoria was an expert in the ways of others, much as Charlotte knew the ways of horses. Her friend had made it her business to know human nature and Charlotte felt certain that she would know just what Lady Clarence's reasoning in this affair might be.

She found Honoria in her father's study, wrapped in blankets and huddled by the fire. Mr. Fitz had taken it upon himself to visit the poorer members of the parish that day and he met Charlotte at the door, wrapped in a large cloak and with a pair of galoshes on his feet and a large hat upon his head.

"You will find Honoria suffering from a chill, I have

put her by the fire, but she will be glad to see you, of that I am certain," the elderly cleric said, smiling at Charlotte as he departed into the snow.

Charlotte made her way to the study, the sounds of sneezing echoing through the house. She looked up with a smile at Charlotte as she entered the room, calling for tea to be brought, as they settled down together by the fire.

"I have had quite an adventure," Charlotte said.

Honoria's attention was immediately pricked.

Charlotte explained what had happened up at Glebe Abbey the night before and how she had come to the aid of the Duke and his horse. Honoria listened in a state of great excitement, as Charlotte explained how she had seen a different side to the Duke, a tender side, without the pretensions which had marred their earlier encounters. At least until the arrival of Lady Clarence.

"Well, it is obvious, is it not?" Honoria said as Charlotte concluded her tale.

"Not to me, that is why I came to see you. If anyone

can explain her strange behavior, I thought it might be you," Charlotte replied.

"I had always wondered as to the speed of your engagement, Charlotte, it seemed somewhat immediate, given your earlier dismissal of the married state," Honoria said, narrowing her eyes and fixing Charlotte with a puzzled expression.

Charlotte sighed. It had been difficult to conceal her true intentions from her closest friend, but she had felt no other choice than to hide the deception from everyone, including Honoria. But now that her feelings for the Duke had been genuinely aroused, she wondered if truthfully, she might marry the Duke in sincerity, rather than as a mere ploy. The thought was attractive, for if he were as taken by horses as she then surely it would be the most ideal match.

"Well, perhaps I was not entirely honest with you," Charlotte said, and then she explained the original arrangement between herself and the Duke, much to Honoria's surprise and amusement.

"I knew it, I knew there was something more to it.

And your mother and father have no idea?" she asked.

Charlotte shrugged her shoulders. "No, none… and they cannot find out. It would be too awful if they did. They need not, especially if… well, if my feelings for the Duke are more sincere than I believed at first," Charlotte said.

"And that is why you have come to seek my opinion?" Honoria's face broke into a smile.

"I just do not understand Lady Clarence's attitude towards me," Charlotte said, for it entirely confused her as to why the Duke's sister should behave in such a way.

"But is it not obvious, Charlotte?" Honoria said, and Charlotte shrugged her shoulders again.

"Not to me," she replied.

"She is jealous of you. You are taking away her brother. She is not married and, from what I have heard, she is not courting and has not done so for some time. She will think that you are trying to snatch her brother away from her and leave her as a lonely spinster. At which point she will feel a burden upon her brother and one you will soon wish to rid Glebe Abbey of when you are Duchess," Honoria said, looking at Charlotte with a triumphant expression.

"Jealous? Do you really think so?" Charlotte asked for it had never occurred to her that Lady Clarence might feel in such a way towards her.

"I know so. It is surely in her nature. But you spend your entire time with the horses, Charlotte, you do not notice such things. I could see it in her face on that day we called upon her. A jealous type but not, I think, without a heart. She cares for her brother and clearly thinks that she is to lose him to you, especially as the contract was transacted so quickly," Honoria said.

Charlotte pondered this for a moment, mulling over Honoria's words. It made sense of course, but what was she to do about it?

"But what course of action should I take? Can Lady Clarence be appeased? I would not wish for the Duke and me to be married without her blessing, but she seems adamant to put a stop to it. She ordered him from the stables today before I could even bid him goodbye," Charlotte said.

"Speak with her, alone. Tell her that you are not a threat, make her see it. She is surely amicable enough to listen, but perhaps not willing to do so at first. If she considers you a threat, then you must make her understand that you are not. It is simple enough, surely," Honoria said, smiling at Charlotte, as she pulled her blanket more tightly around her and glanced out into the snow.

"You are right, Honoria, I knew I could rely on you," Charlotte said, smiling at her friend, who laughed.

"I know nothing of horses, Charlotte. But I know you well enough and I know that your feelings towards the Duke are softening, if only for his love of horses," she replied.

"It is not only that, I saw something entirely different in him when we were alone. A spark, a flame, a true delight. He was not just the Duke, but himself, a man with many attractive qualities. A man I would happily marry, despite my protestations to the contrary," Charlotte said.

She had thought of little else since the night before,

amazed at the transformation which had come over the Duke, amazed at the change in her own feelings. It was as though the healing of the horse had brought healing to herself and to the Duke. They had been brought together on that night in the stable and now Charlotte was determined to make Lady Clarence see that far from being a threat the two of them could surely be friends.

"Then you will go to talk to her?" Honoria asked.

Charlotte nodded. "Immediately," she said, and Honoria smiled, before sneezing loudly.

"And be careful not to catch your death of cold," she said, sneezing once again.

Back out in the snow, Charlotte made her way quickly towards the lane leading to Glebe Abbey. She would call upon Lady Clarence but before that, she wished to see the Duke's horse and check if it had passed a comfortable morning. She had no doubt that her ministrations had been effective and that the horse was now almost fully recovered, but she had a strange desire to see it, especially as it was the Duke's favorite.

The snow had been shoveled in the stable yard, cleared to either side, and several members of the house staff were feeding pails of oats and sections of hay to the horses. Charlotte made her way to the far end of the yard, hoping that she might perhaps find the Duke himself there tending to the horse. But, as she approached the door, she found it half-open, a voice coming from inside. It was that of Lady Clarence and she paused just outside, not wishing to disturb her.

"I am sorry my dear thing, I should have known what to do to help you. I felt so inadequate, I should have known, I was a failure," Lady Clarence sounded so sad, and Charlotte peered cautiously around the door.

There, she saw the Duke's sister standing by the side of the horse, gently stroking its neck. Her head was bowed, but the horse seemed entirely cured, no longer sweating or in distress, but happily chomping of some sweet hay.

"There is no failure, Lady Clarence, the horse is well

and that is all that matters. I am sure you did everything you could," Charlotte said, and Lady Clarence looked up with a scowl.

"I... oh, no... you do not understand," Lady Clarence started.

"I think I do," Charlotte replied, "and if I do not then perhaps you will tell me," she said, smiling at the lady and coming to stroke Brack's neck opposite Lady Clarence.

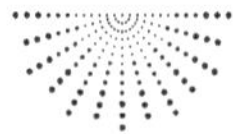

CHAPTER TEN

Lady Clarence sighed, looking at the horse and gently stroking his neck. She glanced at Charlotte, who continued to smile, waiting for her to speak.

"I longed to enter the veterinary school in Lyon, my French is excellent, but I was told it was a vain fancy. A lady such as I does not do a thing like that," she said, shaking her head sadly.

Charlotte was taken aback for a moment, she had not expected such a revelation for Lady Clarence had never shown any such inclination.

"Then you are just like I, Lady Clarence. My only

ambition has been to enter such a happy state and learn all I could about the veterinary arts. But I was forbidden too. Time and again I was forbidden it. Marriage to your brother is perhaps the only way I might achieve my dream. But you should have every opportunity," Charlotte said, reaching out and placing her hand upon that of Lady Clarence.

"But I do not have your learning, Miss Botley. When I saw you here this morning it grieved me deeply. I knew that your skills far surpassed my own. As did your determination, you didn't let being forbidden stop you from learning... I did," Lady Clarence replied, as the horse gave a whinny and blew out a great stream of warm breath.

"Everything I have learned has come from the pages of books in my father's library. I have had no formal education, the most I have learned has come from Michael, my father's groom. He has taught me what he knows, and I have tried my best to learn as best I could. I had no idea of your interest though, Lady Clarence, and would gladly share everything I know. It would be a delight to do so, to talk to someone with a similar interest. We do not have to be rivals," Charlotte said.

Lady Clarence looked at her in surprise. "I have no rivals," she said, her tone sounding curt and somewhat offended.

"But you must admit that you and I have not been on the best of terms since my engagement to your brother. You have been entirely cold towards me and shown no attempt or effort to make me welcome," Charlotte said.

"Because I do not want him to be taken away from me. He is all I have, and the suddenness of your engagement startled me. When he told me of it I was quite shocked," Lady Clarence said, still stroking the horse's head, though she now looked at Charlotte with the merest hint of a tear in her eye.

"Lady Clarence, I have no desire to take your brother from you. He is a dear and gentle man and you are quite his equal, at least when you want to be," Charlotte replied.

Lady Clarence looked at her and smiled, her head on one side, as she let out a sigh.

"I had always so longed to be a horseman, a foolish thing I know. But how I love to ride out and to ride out with Sebastian. Knowing that you too shared such a passion quite put me ill at ease. I imagined the two of you riding out and leaving me all alone at the house, I would have nothing, no happiness at all," she said, shaking her head.

"But that is not true. I have no desire to exclude you. Indeed, the thought of a sister in law such as you quite overwhelms me. You would be most welcome to join in my studies and to learn from Michael too. We could learn together, all of us, your brother too," Charlotte said, beginning to imagine the wonderful possibility which now appeared to have opened up.

"I should like that very much, Miss Botley," Lady Clarence said, and her face now broke into the most delightful smile.

Charlotte nodded, reaching out and taking her by the hands, laying them on the horse's neck and feeling for its temperature.

"There now, this horse is well and not only from my ministrations. I can see that you have that same gift which Michael has too, the gift of the whisper. The horse is listening to you, he understands you. He understands that you are a friend to him," Charlotte said, and Lady Clarence beamed a warm smile.

"Do you really think so?" she asked.

Charlotte nodded. "It is clear to see, Lady Clarence, as clear as the day," Charlotte said, just as a noise at the stable door caused them to turn.

It was the Duke and he looked entirely bemused to see the two women stood side by side next to the horse.

"Miss Botley was just explaining my ability with the horses," Lady Clarence said, as the Duke entered the stable.

"I have always said that you are the most effective at calming them and alleviating their nerves," the Duke replied.

"I am a whisperer, and Miss Botley has invited me to study with her," Lady Clarence said, her entire demeanor having changed.

"Then you are on friendly terms now?" the Duke asked, and his sister nodded.

"I am sorry that I stood in your way. I have been such

a terrible fool, Sebastian. I believe that Miss Botley would take you away from me and that I would be left with nothing but my broken dreams. But I am reassured that such a thing is not to be," Lady Clarence said.

The Duke came to stand in the straw and patted the horse's neck. He glanced at Charlotte, who blushed a little, but smiled at him and he nodded, beaming at them both in turn.

"Then you will cease this silliness and no longer forbid me from telling Miss Botley how I truly feel?" he asked.

"I will," she replied.

Sebastian turned to Charlotte, taking her by the hand.

"I am sorry for the way you have been treated, Charlotte. I had no desire to hurt Emily by our engagement, for I knew she thought that if you and I were close then our closeness as brother and sister would soon fall to the wayside. I was so anxious to share my love of horses with you, for I knew you shared it too and that we could be the happiest of people together. But I also had no desire to hurt

Emily or to make her think that anything would change between us. Can you forgive me?" he asked.

Charlotte laughed. "But surely you must both have realized that I am nothing like that. To think that I might have discovered two people who share the same love and passion as I is quite beyond belief. I would have embraced you both and ensured that the three of us could be the best of friends," Charlotte said, almost laughing in amazement at this new revelation.

"Last night, I saw that I could never hope to hide my true feelings for you. I have fallen entirely in love with you, though I have perhaps done a better job of showing myself as foolish rather than loving," the Duke replied.

"Though that is entirely my fault, Miss Botley," Lady Clarence said, "I begged Sebastian not to grow close to you. I know he does not really wish to marry, I have always known it, no doubt he believed he should do so. But I soon learned that his feelings for you were growing and, in my foolishness, I tried to stand in his way."

Charlotte glanced at the Duke and it seemed pointless

to reveal the true nature of their arrangement. She smiled at him, knowing that in fact her feelings now ran far deeper than a simple arrangement of convenience. No longer did she wish to marry the Duke so that her ambitions might be fulfilled, but instead she wished to marry him for the simple fact that he was a kindred spirit and, in the stable that last night, she had seen his true self shine through.

"And my feelings for you are the same," Charlotte whispered, causing a broad smile to break over his face, as he blushed in the chill of the cold morning air.

"Then we will surely be the best of friends now," Lady Clarence said, and the Duke nodded.

"And Charlotte and I will marry, without obstacle or difficulty?" he asked, and Lady Clarence smiled.

"It seems that we have all had a drastic change of heart this past night," she said, taking Charlotte by the hand, "come now, I think it is high time for some tea, do you not?"

"An excellent suggestion," the Duke said, offering Charlotte his arm.

Lady Clarence hurried off across the stable yard, as Charlotte smiled at the Duke and shook her head.

"You could have told me this, we could have saved ourselves a great deal of trouble," she said, as they walked arm in arm towards the house.

"I was a fool. I thought like you that I did not wish to marry. I had no interest or desire in it, no thought to it. But when I came to realize the affinity which we had for one another, my whole vision was quite changed. But I hated to see Emily upset, I am all she has you see," he said.

Charlotte shook her head. "She has me now, and I am sure we shall be the closest of friends," Charlotte replied, and with a smile, the Duke leaned down and kissed her upon the cheek.

"How glad I am to hear you say that and how glad I am that at last, I can tell you how very much I have fallen in love with you, even if I tried my best not to show it," he replied, causing her to laugh.

"I was somewhat reticent myself, but you have shown me that it is possible not only to find a man who shares my passions, but who can cause me to change my mind entirely. Marriage now seems a most attractive proposition," she said.

"Then let us make no delay," he said, and together they hurried towards the house, each having finally realized the true feelings of their hearts.

CHAPTER ELEVEN

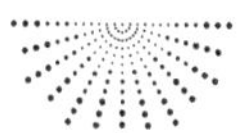

It was December and the wedding of Charlotte and the Duke was to take place just a week before Christmas. The autumnal storms had given way to a most delightful season of crisp and cold weather, the snow lay upon the ground and the sky blue and bright above. They were to be married by Mr. Fitz, for the Duke did not share his uncle's religious sensibilities, and the service would be followed by a lavish banquet at Glebe Abbey, to which the whole district had been invited.

Charlotte's mother and father had been surprised to find her so strangely enthused by the prospect of her wedding. She had returned from Glebe Abbey on that fateful afternoon some months previously accompanied by the Duke and immediately engaged her mother in a conversation as to the details of her wedding. Her mother and father were none the wiser as to the details of the arrangement between Charlotte and the Duke, but that hardly mattered now that they had found the true love they each deserved.

Both Charlotte and the Duke had discovered in one another the happy coincidence of a shared and lifelong passion. A fact which is surely a promising beginning to any marriage, and, in Lady Clarence, Charlotte had found a new and intimate friend. She and Honoria were quick to welcome Lady Clarence into their circle and even Honoria had to admit that the prospect of learning more about horses was something she found attractive.

Together, they had spent much time in the stables of Goodnell Manor and at Glebe Abbey, tending to the horses and sharing their knowledge. Michael was an excellent teacher of the practicalities and Charlotte did her best to teach the others everything she had learned from her books. There seemed little need for further thoughts of the veterinary school, given that

Charlotte appeared to possess all the knowledge necessary to be the finest of the practitioners in her field. She was an expert and there was no doubting that what she did not know about horses was really not worth knowing.

It was Honoria who assisted Charlotte in preparing for her wedding day. She had insisted upon riding to the church, much to her mother and father's bemusement and, in a marked break with tradition, she had decided to ride alongside the Duke who would arrive at Goodnell Manor at eleven o'clock. Now, she was dressed in a most elegant white wedding gown, trimmed with lace and covered by a red velvet cloak against the cold.

"You look oh so beautiful, Charlotte," Honoria said, as she stepped back to admire Charlotte's outfit.

"As do you, Honoria, our cloaks match, as do our smiles," Charlotte said, embracing her friend and kissing her on both cheeks.

"This is such a happy day, Charlotte. I never thought I would see you married. I thought we were destined to eternal spinsterhood together," Honoria said, adjusting one final part of Charlotte's dress.

"You shall soon find a husband, Honoria. If I, who was so intent upon not finding one can do so, then there is every hope that you will do so," Charlotte said, as a knock came at the door.

Sir Cyril had come to escort the two women downstairs to where the horses were waiting. He had not inherited his own father's love for the equestrian, nor did he share his daughter's passions. He and Charlotte's mother would travel together in a carriage behind the happy couple, the Duke having just arrived to escort his bride to the church.

"The Duke is here now, Charlotte. You do look ever so beautiful, just as your mother and I always imagined you would do on your wedding day," Charlotte's father said, and he embraced Charlotte, before taking her by the arm and escorting the two friends downstairs.

Charlotte's mother was waiting for them in the hallway, dressed in the finery of a mother of the bride and protected from the chill by a cloak of blue velvet and a matching bonnet. She beamed at Charlotte, all sense of worry and concern now gone from her countenance, replaced with just the simple delight of a mother who is about to see her only daughter married.

"What a truly happy day this is, Charlotte. The happiest of days. Come now, the Duke is waiting," she said, as the maid opened the door and the party stepped out onto the forecourt before Goodnell Manor.

There, a carriage sat, resplendent with liveried horses and in front of that was the Duke, mounted upon the stead which he and Charlotte had so carefully tended together. At his side was Chaser, equally well-attired and appearing impatient to transport her mistress to the church.

"The carriage awaits, and your ride is prepared," the Duke said, smiling at Charlotte, as he looked at her in delight.

"Sidesaddle, Charlotte," her mother said, as Charlotte hurried towards the horse and the Duke leaped down to help her up. "It was your previous posture which so detracted from your better qualities."

"Mother, really, I have always ridden in the seemliest

of manners," Charlotte replied, and her mother laughed.

Soon, Charlotte was seated elegantly upon Chaser's back, her red cloak wrapped around her dress, standing out against the white and blue backdrop of that perfect winter morning. Charlotte's mother and father, along with Honoria. Sat in the carriage, as the party departed, led by the Duke. They rode in procession towards the church and there was much delight and merrymaking as they went along. The route was lined with deckings of holly as the village prepared to celebrate Christmas and the whole feeling was magical.

As they approached the church, Charlotte could see Mr. Fitz awaiting them at the lychgate, surrounded by a sizeable crowd of well-wishers. He greeted them, as the horses and carriage drew up, the crowd giving a round of applause, as the Duke helped Charlotte down from her horse.

"It seems that the whole village has turned out to wish us well," the Duke said, beaming around at the crowds.

"God bless you both, Your Grace," called out one of the women, and the sentiment was passed around.

Charlotte looked around her for Emily, for she had thought that she too would ride in procession with them. To her great surprise, she saw her at the door of the church, but she was not alone, and instead, her arm was linked with Michael, the two of them waving to Charlotte and the Duke with much enthusiasm.

"Did you know of this?" Charlotte asked, as she took the Duke's arm and they followed Mr. Fitz into the church.

"Not a whisper," he said, as they passed by Emily and Michael, who seemed entirely at ease and delight in one another's company.

"Then today we celebrate not one, but two happy meetings," Charlotte replied.

The crowds now filed into the church, following Charlotte and the Duke who was led towards the front of the church by Mr. Fitz, with Honoria acting as a bridesmaid. Charlotte had done away with traditional convention, though her father had insisted upon presenting her to the Duke before the service began. This he did with some ceremony, telling the Duke that he was receiving something of a free spirit, as Mr. Fitz opened his prayer book.

"And now, on this happy day, we come to celebrate the joyous moment of marriage," he said, peering at Charlotte and the Duke over his glasses with a smile, as the wedding rites began.

As the bells of the church rang out and Charlotte and the Duke shared their first kiss as man and wife, a great cheer went up from the congregation and the organ thundered into a magnificent wedding march. Charlotte and the Duke walked arm in arm down the aisle, congratulated upon all sides by well-wishers from near and far.

At the door to the church, they met Emily and Michael, still on one another's arms and beaming broadly. They appeared as happy as Charlotte and the Duke, and it seemed that their friendship had bloomed into romance, thanks to the passions which they shared. They could only thank Charlotte and the Duke for bringing them together, a joy which would surely lead to yet more happiness to come.

"But Emily, you told me nothing of this newfound

happiness," the Duke said, as Emily and Michael laughed.

"You had so much else to think of, Sebastian. Besides, we wanted to surprise you both. We have something else to tell you too, we intend to travel to London and seek instruction at the veterinary school. There is much still to learn and together we want to know all that we can," Emily said, as Charlotte let out a cry of delight.

"How wonderful for you both and what a happy joy that shall be," she said, as Emily glanced at Michael and back to Charlotte.

"You do not think it an impertinence upon my part, Charlotte?" she asked, and Charlotte shook her head.

"No, dear Emily, of course, I do not. Sebastian and I have spoken much on this matter and we feel that in marriage our place is here. I have already learned so much and to abandon all that is here simply to pursue my own fancy seems wrong. You must gain the knowledge and then return to share it with us. Together we shall make something wonderful here, I am certain," Charlotte replied.

"Come now, is there not a feast to enjoy?"

Charlotte's father said, coming up behind them, with a smile upon his face.

"Yes, a marvelous feast, come now. We shall ride back to Glebe Abbey and enjoy it," the Duke said, kissing Charlotte before leading her down the steps of the church to where the horses were waiting patiently in the snow.

G lebe Abbey had never known such a crowd to crowd its interiors. The Duke and his sister had ensured that everywhere was decorated with greenery and that every fire and lamp and candle was burning brightly so that the celebrations could go on long into the evening. A magnificent Christmas tree held pride of place as you came into the house. Charlotte knew that she would never have a Christmas as magical as this one. Before she entered the Duke picked her up and carried her over the threshold, stopping and looking up as he crossed into the hall.

Charlotte waited and eventually looked up to and saw that he was holding her under a sprig of mistletoe. With a smile, she closed her eyes and felt his lips on hers. A tingle went through her and she leaned into the kiss. This really was the best Christmas ever.

"I must put you down or we will be trampled," Sebastian whispered into her ear. "Don't worry, I will save some kisses for later."

"You'd better," she whispered before stealing another kiss from his lips.

A lavish feast had been prepared and laid out in the dining room and there was to be dancing in the long gallery and music throughout the day.

The horses had been safely stabled, and the wedding party now made its way back into the house, just as the carriages began to arrive at the forecourt. Charlotte waited to greet her mother and father who came once again to congratulate her and offer their hopes for her future. Her mother was beaming, and she embraced Charlotte, showering her with kisses.

"How happy we are, Charlotte. What a happy day

this is," she said, and Sir Cyril expressed a similar sentiment.

"I should never have thought that such a thing would be the case. We had thought you would never marry, my dear daughter, that you would never find happiness."

"But I was happy, father. I was happy with everything I had, but I discovered that it was possible to be even happier when one shares one's passions with another," Charlotte replied, and they both smiled.

"You are saying that if it were not for the horses then this happy day would not have occurred," her father asked, raising his eyebrows.

Charlotte smiled and tilted her head to one side. "I could not possibly say, father," she replied, and he laughed.

"Then perhaps now is the time to offer a toast to your equine friends. They have given me much trouble over the years and many sleepless nights to your dear mother but it seems we should have trusted them to make things right, for certainly, they have." He ushered Charlotte and her mother to the side, where the waiting guests were assembled.

"Your mother and father seem pleased," the Duke said, as he kissed Charlotte on the cheek.

"I think they have rather come around to our way of thinking," Charlotte said, and she proceeded to tell the Duke all about it, much to his amusement.

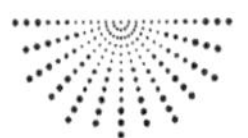

utumn came late to Glebe Abbey, in contrast to the previous year, and Charlotte was delivered of a child, a healthy boy, with hair just his like his father's and eyes just like his mother's. He was an energetic baby, who they named Rupert after Charlotte's grandfather. That did not prevent Charlotte from ensuring that he was quickly introduced to the horses, taking him to the stables at Glebe Abbey just as soon as it was safe to do so.

"A child can never meet a horse too early," she said, as she and the Duke walked across the cobbles towards the stable yard.

They had enjoyed the happiest of times together

since their wedding, delighting in one another's company and settling into the routines of married life. In contrast to her mother's predictions, Charlotte had found the running of Glebe Abbey to be a matter of some simplicity.

The house had been so devoid of organization under its previous occupant that Charlotte had found the servants largely used to making their own arrangements. This had given her ample time to make the stables her own and she had brought many of the horses from Goodnell Manor to stable at the Abbey as well as some of the staff.

Her father had not minded in the least, particularly as he had lost his groom to a marriage to Lady Clarence. The two of them had traveled to the veterinary school in London but were due to return that very day, their short course of study now complete. Emily had written often to Charlotte, telling her in some amazement just how little was known of the sciences which they took for granted.

"I am looking forward to seeing Emily and Michael. They are such a happy couple together," the Duke said.

"And they shall see the baby for the first time too, I am sure it shall arouse the most maternal of instincts in Emily," Charlotte said, smiling at the Duke and peering down at Rupert, asleep in her arms.

"Do you think they shall stay? Or will they set off for London again?" Sebastian asked as they came to the stables.

"I hope they shall stay, we have much work for them here," Charlotte said, looking proudly around her at what she and the Duke had created.

A new stable block was being built and the couple had plans to breed thoroughbreds for racing, hoping to produce the finest steads in all of England. But to do so, they would need the help and expertise of Michael and Emily, not to mention their own abilities too.

"But now, it is time to introduce Rupert to his new friends, I think," the Duke said, as they turned to where the horses were stabled, making their way to one particular door.

"Rupert, you must meet your father's favorite horse," Charlotte said, as the baby stirred in her arms.

He opened his eyes and let out a yawn, his fingers curling around her own, as she lifted him gently to see over into the stable.

"I am not sure he is quite as interested as his parents may at first have believed," the Duke said, laughing and shaking his head.

"He is only a month old," Charlotte replied, smiling at Sebastian, as she brought Rupert back to her breast and kissed him gently upon the forehead.

"Will he be a racer or a trainer? Will he sit astride and ride or will he breed the most wonderful champions here in his father's stable," the Duke asked, as he stepped through the door to stroke his favorite horse's mane.

"Or perhaps he will be a healer like his mother and his aunt," Charlotte retorted.

"Whatever he becomes I want him only to be happy and always true to himself, it is the only way to be," the Duke replied.

They led the horse out into the stable yard, where several of the others were now gathered for their exercise. It was a fine sight to behold and Charlotte could not help but feel proud at all they had achieved together. Soon, they would have a stable to rival any in England and horses worthy of the Regent's stable itself.

"To think, we might have the greatest of champions here in our midst, a thoroughbred to challenge any that the Regent may possess. Think of it, how wonderful it would be," Charlotte said, as the sound of a carriage could be heard on the forecourt of the house.

"And this is surely Emily and Michael now arrived," Sebastian said, and the two of them hurried off excitedly to greet their guests.

"The wanderers have returned," Charlotte said, as Michael and Emily stepped down from the carriage.

The former groom had grown a beard and Emily seemed to have blossomed in the joys of married life, so much so that Charlotte looked at her with some curiosity.

"You are right to look, for we have wonderful news," Emily said, as Charlotte let out a cry of delight.

"Then Rupert is to have a cousin?" she asked, and

Emily nodded.

"In the new year and we have come to share the happy news that we intend to raise the child here at Glebe Abbey. We are tired of London, it is not as we imagined. They know nothing, absolutely nothing of horsemanship," Emily said, turning to Michael, who nodded.

"It is quite true. There is little that they could teach us, in fact, we found ourselves often called upon to impart our knowledge to them. You would have been bored from the very first instant, Charlotte. If anyone should open a veterinary school then it is you," Michael said, as the four of them exchanged their greetings.

Charlotte blushed, the thought of such a thing quite taking her breath away. Her entire life had been spent in dreaming of the veterinary school, but the reports she had received from Emily and Michael had turned such dreams into something quite different. She did not need anyone to tell her how best to take care of a horse, for she had come to realize that she already knew it all herself, more so than anyone else, thanks entirely to her own hard work and dedication.

"But come now, you must allow us to meet our dear nephew properly, Charlotte and to see the stables," Emily said, placing a gentle finger upon Rupert's lips, as the baby stirred and began to squirm in Charlotte's arms.

"Why not take him for a moment and walk on to the stables, we shall catch you up," Charlotte said, passing the baby to her sister in law, and linking arms with Sebastian.

"They seem entirely happy in one another's company," Sebastian said, as he and Charlotte followed Emily and Michael towards the stables.

"They have found true love and who could not be happy in that?" Charlotte replied, as she leaned on Sebastian's arm and rested her head upon his shoulder.

"And by such a happy coincidence too," the Duke said, turning and placing a gentle kiss upon her forehead.

"Did you ever imagine yourself to be truly happy?" Charlotte asked, and he shook his head.

"I thought I knew what happiness was. I thought it to

be the making of my own ends, my own dreams, my own destiny. Happiness was to be found upon my own terms and no one else's. I never imagined that it might be the result of someone else. Of another's influence," he replied.

"I thought just the same, I believed I had found happiness in precisely what I wanted it to be. Not in another. But then all of that was changed," she said.

"How fortunate to find a kindred spirit, someone who truly understands how one is, someone to share one's whole life with," the Duke replied.

"Whatever Rupert shall be he will know one thing and that is that he shall always make his own decisions, that much I can promise," Charlotte said, as they came into the stable yard and watched as Emily and Michael carried the baby proudly around to see the horses.

"Even if he decides he would rather not ride a horse in all his life?" the Duke asked, turning and grinning at her.

Charlotte paused for a moment and smiled.

"He will most certainly wish to ride but if he does

not then I hope he will do precisely what we did and stand up for himself. Happiness is worth that, is it not?" she said, and the Duke nodded, as the sound of the neighing horses echoed over the stable yard.

"It is worth it a thousand times over," he said, and taking her in his arms he kissed her, in the delightful knowledge that they had found their happiness by staying true to themselves and coming to know the passions of the other, a passion which would last a lifetime.

If you enjoyed this book I have a new box set out with some of my author friends. It is 32 Sweet Romances and you can grab 32 Beautiful Brides and Bouncing Babies here

"Now then, we really must start packing. I know we shall not be leaving until Friday, but one can never be too well prepared," Lady Ariadne Milford said as she heaved herself to her feet with her customary noisy groan. "Goodness, old age is catching up with me."

"Shall I ask the housekeeper to have your wooden trunk laid out in your room, My Lady?" Jane asked and hoped that she was being helpful. "And then, perhaps, you could tell me what you need, and I could help you pack."

"Not at all, my dear. The housekeeper has everything under control and my lady's maid will pack for me. She is well versed on my traveling needs, Jane." Lady Ariadne gave Jane a reassuring smile. "No, I think you and I shall take tea instead and discuss this nephew of mine. I daresay it will be of some use to you to know a little something of him before we arrive at Sotheby Hall." She looked across the drawing room to the bell rope hanging neatly by the side of the chimney breast. "I know it is early, my dear, but what-say you ring for tea anyway?"

"Of course, Lady Ariadne," Jane said and dutifully rose from her perch on the couch and silently hurried across the room.

"My dear, you are always so keen to help with everything." Lady Ariadne was studying Jane as she made her way back across the room. "But you really are only my companion, Jane. You must try not to be one of my servants, for you are not. I know the circumstances of your father's passing have made you nervous, but you are still a well-bred young woman. None of us know in our youth how the world is going to treat us, but we always have our breeding to fall back upon."

"You are very kind, Lady Ariadne." Jane settled back on the very edge of the couch opposite her mistress.

"Oh, do sit comfortably, Jane. You make me feel as if there is some emergency that I am not yet aware of." Lady Ariadne waved her companion back into her seat. "That's it, lean back a little at least. Is that not more comfortable?"

"Yes, thank you," Jane said and wished she could find some way to feel at her ease.

But her life had been turned upside down with the passing of her father and she felt like a fish out of water.

Her father, Lord Briars, a baron, had struggled for most of his life with a failing estate, doing everything in his power to see it continue for generations to come, even if his heir was to be his nephew. Jane had been his only child and his only relief had been to know that his nephew would have happily kept Jane safe on the estate when the time came. But when the time did come, there was nothing left for Jane's cousin to inherit and no way for that fine young man to add her to his already great responsibilities. In the end, Jane had taken matters into her own hands and struck out into the world in search of a job. Thinking first to try for a position as a governess, she had found luck at last when the very first post she had been offered had been as a companion to Lady Ariadne Milford. It was better paid and kept her status at least a bit better elevated than if she had become a governess.

"Now then, about my nephew," Lady Ariadne began, bringing Jane back into the here and now. "I have not yet told you much about him. The truth is that I did not think he would agree to see me and so I thought there was little point in giving you any of the details before now."

"I see," Jane said, not really seeing but feeling she ought to add to the conversation in some way.

It wouldn't do for her to simply smile benignly and stare out of one of Brockett Hall's ceiling-height windows or to admire the largest fireplace she had ever seen. Lady Ariadne liked her companion to be just that; a companion. She was expected to participate, to give opinions, even offer advice on occasion. But with a woman of such a forceful character as Lady Ariadne, such confidence was not easily found.

"Oh, but he was such a dear boy to me, Jane. Such a handsome little lad." Lady Ariadne looked suddenly upset and Jane, unused to dealing with such things, began to fear she had no means by which to manage. "And when he set off for Spain, his father and me pleading with him to reconsider, he was so full of enthusiasm for life and everything in it." Quite out of the blue, Lady Ariadne dabbed at her eyes with a handkerchief.

"Lady Ariadne, what is it? What is upsetting you?" Jane, feeling certain that her mistress would not want her to dash across the room and comfort her physically, decided to get to the heart of the matter.

After all, it was Lady Ariadne's way of doing things and Jane could only hope that she would appreciate a little forthrightness.

"Oh, I am upset my dear. Very upset. I am always this way when I think of my poor dear Nathaniel."

"Your nephew? But why?"

"He was so terribly wounded out there in Spain. Oh, how I wish he would never have gone."

"Lady Ariadne, forgive me, but is your nephew an invalid on account of his wounds? Is that why you are so upset?" Jane spoke gently.

"No, he is not an invalid, except that he makes himself so." Lady Ariadne, just as her character dictated, sniffed in a loud and unladylike manner without apology, forcing Jane to stifle an inappropriate laugh.

"I do not understand."

"He has made himself a recluse. That handsome boy who left home at just twenty is now a man of thirty who might just as well live in a cave for all the people he sees. He has made himself a hermit."

"And that is why you did not think he would agree to your visit?"

"Yes." Lady Ariadne blew her nose with all the grace of a farmhand. "But he has, and so I must be pleased. And I am, although I suppose it is true to say I am more relieved than anything. I have not seen him for two years. Before that it was three." She shrugged. "I just hope that he will let me help him this time. Let *us* help him," she said and looked meaningfully at Jane.

As Jane smiled kindly, she wondered just what was going to be expected of her.

"I suppose you must prepare a room for my aunt, Mrs. Marlow. It seems that she will not be denied this time." Nathaniel Alexander, the Earl of Sotheby, gave his housekeeper a defeated sigh.

"Very good, My Lord. And I shall have servants' rooms aired and ready for the lady's maid and the driver." The middle-aged housekeeper nodded slowly. "Is Lady Milford to bring anyone further, My Lord?"

"Not that I am aware of. Was that the extent of her entourage on her last visit? I can hardly remember, Mrs. Marlow."

"Yes, My Lord. Just the two servants."

"Then I suppose that is all we can prepare for." She shrugged. "My aunt is a creature of habit; I daresay she will bring the same two servants with her."

"Very well, My Lord. Will that be all?"

"Yes, thank you. I will not be needing anything else this evening," he smiled at Mrs. Marlow, letting her know she was free to get on with whatever she chose to do for the rest of the evening.

For his part, Nathaniel had already decided that a few glasses of brandy in front of the fire would serve him very nicely. He had picked out a book which he had already laid out on the side table next to his fireside armchair, although he knew he was unlikely to read a word of it.

As was common when he had something on his mind, Nathaniel would simply sit and drink by the fire with the open book on his lap and no idea of the story contained within its pages.

No sooner was the door closed than Nathaniel was on his feet approaching the drinks trolley. Even as he poured his first large serving of brandy, he could still hear the departing footsteps of Mrs. Marlow.

With a sigh, he took his glass back to the fireside and settled heavily down in the armchair, its thick blue brocade upholstery rough and pleasingly unyielding as he tried to make himself comfortable. He smiled; he liked that. Life was not easy, not even making oneself comfortable, and he did not want it to be either.

Nathaniel wanted to remind himself every day of the foolishness he had once been so guilty of. The foolishness which had made him such a bright and optimistic young man and sent him off to war all those years ago as if it was nothing more than a boy's adventure. He wanted to be reminded of his mistake every day. Not so that he never made it again, for he knew that the young man he had once been would never return. No, it was so that he could remind himself exactly who was to blame for his current life; the life which would be his until he was finally tipped into the grave.

The scars which covered his right upper body and part of his face had been his doing. His self-imposed exile from the world had been his doing. His loneliness had been his doing.

It seemed to Nathaniel that even his loneliness was not enough to make him truly want the company of his aunt, nor anybody else. The only people he could bear to see were his staff, and only because they were so used to his appearance that they never gave any indication that something was amiss.

They had at first, of course, but how could they not have? He had left Sotheby Hall as a handsome man of twenty with all the arrogance of youth. He had returned a very different man just two years later, a man who would bear the scars of his foolhardy youth for the rest of his life.

The staff at Sotheby had, by nothing more than familiarity, grown used to their master as he was now, and it had been a relief to him that his beloved father had passed before he had returned from the war.

It had broken his heart, for Nathaniel had loved his father, but he loved him so much that he could not have suffered to see the effect his altered appearance would have had on him. His aunt's devastation had been more than enough.

Still, Lady Ariadne was a tough old soul and she was much better able to hide her sadness these days, even if she could not hide it completely. It was not as if she was going to be seeing him afresh; she would not gape at him the way strangers or even acquaintances did whenever he chanced to leave the walls and grounds of Sotheby.

"Oh, perhaps I will enjoy the company," he said to himself rather loudly before gulping down every drop of brandy in the glass. "Perhaps this visit will be a good thing."

He leaned back in his armchair, feeling the rough brocade beneath his flattened palm, and stared into the flames.

Nathaniel knew, of course, that his beloved aunt could not help but try to find some way to help him. He knew she could not bear the idea of his self-determined seclusion and would try everything in her power to drag him out into the world again.

She was a strong old thing and she certainly took some fending off. Nathaniel shook his head and realized he was smiling; not a thing he did very often.

Perhaps it was time to let her in just a little, she loved him dearly after all.

"Perhaps," he said to himself again as he rose to pour himself another brandy. "Perhaps."

Read The Dance of Love for FREE with Kindle Unlimited

FREE The Shallow Waters of Romance

Get a FREE eBook and find out about Charlotte's new releases by joining her newsletter here. Your information will never be shared.

All Books FREE with Kindle Unlimited

40 Sweet Inspirational Romances

Regency Romantic Dreams

A Housekeeper for the Duke

Perfect Harmony with the Lord

Saving the Rake

And many more...

To find all of Charlotte's books, Follow her on Amazon. Just click the yellow follow button when you get to Amazon and they will send you details of special offers and new releases.

I hope you enjoyed these books by Charlotte Darcy.

Charlotte is a hopeless romantic. She loves historical romance and the Regency era the most. She has been a writer for many years and can think of nothing better than seeing how her characters can find their happy ever after.

She lives in Derbyshire, England and when not writing you will find her walking the British countryside with her dog Poppy or visiting stately homes, such as Chatsworth House which is local to her.

You can contact Charlotte at CharlotteDarcy@cd2.com or via Facebook at @CharlotteDarcyAuthor

Or join my exclusive newsletter for a free book and updates on new releases here.